"Watch out!" Sam shouted.

Christy's eyes shot open and she spun in her seat to look around her. A truck was roaring up behind them.

Slam!

"He hit us!" Christy screamed. Her breath caught as a man in a leather jacket with a black beard leaned out the passenger-side window. He seemed to struggle for a moment, then he pulled out a rifle.

"Sam!" she yelled, already unbuckling herself and Ellie and dragging them down to the floor of the back seat.

The rear window shattered, accompanied by Ellie's terrified shrieks. Glass rained down on them. Christy drew her daughter toward her, curving her body around the child.

There was a second shot.

The SUV started to spiral out of control.

Between the blown-out wheel and the incredible speed, the vehicle slid and spun across the road and then collided with a car.

The air was filled with a sharp whoosh as the airbags in the front seat deployed. Sam groaned and the vehicle creaked as it rocked to a stop.

Would the man in the leather jacket come and finish them off?

Dana R. Lynn grew up in Illinois. She met her husband at a wedding and told her parents she'd met the man she was going to marry. Nineteen months later, they were married. Today, they live in rural Pennsylvania with their three children and a variety of animals. In addition to writing, she works as a teacher for the deaf and hard of hearing and is active in her church.

Books by Dana R. Lynn

Love Inspired Suspense

Amish Country Justice

Plain Target
Plain Retribution
Amish Christmas Abduction
Amish Country Ambush
Amish Christmas Emergency
Guarding the Amish Midwife
Hidden in Amish Country
Plain Refuge
Deadly Amish Reunion
Amish Country Threats
Covert Amish Investigation
Amish Christmas Escape

Visit the Author Profile page at LoveInspired.com.

AMISH CHRISTMAS ESCAPE

DANA R. LYNN

LOVE INSPIRED SUSPENSE
INSPIRATIONAL ROMANCE

LOVE INSPIRED® SUSPENSE
INSPIRATIONAL ROMANCE

ISBN-13: 978-1-335-55469-7

Amish Christmas Escape

Copyright © 2021 by Dana Roae

Recycling programs
for this product may
not exist in your area.

This edition published by arrangement with Harlequin Books S.A.

For questions and comments about the quality of this book, please contact us at CustomerService@Harlequin.com.

Love Inspired
22 Adelaide St. West, 40th Floor
Toronto, Ontario M5H 4E3, Canada
www.LoveInspired.com

Printed in U.S.A.

But they that wait upon the Lord shall renew their strength;
they shall mount up with wings as eagles; they shall run,
and not be weary; and they shall walk, and not faint.
—*Isaiah* 40:31

To Amy and Dee. Coffee is always better
when you drink it with your best friends.

Acknowledgments

This past year has been challenging to say the least.
I am so grateful to so many for their unwavering love
and support.

To my husband and children: You are my world. I love
you all forever.

To my parents and brothers: I love you so much.
Thanks for your unconditional support.

Rachel and Lee: You ladies are the best! Thanks for the
sympathy.

The Suspense Squad: I love you ladies! It's great talking
murder and mayhem with y'all.

To my LIS/LI writer friends: I appreciate the advice,
support and, of course, the never-ending supply of
memes.

To my editor, Tina, and my agent, Tamela: I appreciate
you so much. I'm a better writer because of your
unending support.

And most of all, to my Lord and Savior: I pray that my
words always bring You glory.

ONE

"You can take a break." Christina O'Malley, known as Christy to her family, smiled at the evening nurse. "I'll sit with her for a few minutes."

The woman frowned for a second before nodding and vacating her seat beside her patient. Christy waited until the nurse had left her sister's bedroom before slipping into the chair beside the bed.

The door closed. Christy sank back against the cushion and closed her eyes. Something about the woman made her teeth ache. She was forever asking questions. They sounded like casual chatter, but Christy couldn't shake the feeling that there was something deeper than idle curiosity.

She opened her eyes and deliberately turned her gaze away from the elaborately decorated windows. Their house looked like it was straight out of a Christmas catalog rather than a normal family home in Columbus, Ohio. Her stepmother, Vanessa McCormick O'Malley, was obsessed with appearances. There were lights in every window, and three lavish Christmas trees. Even the yard hosted numerous decorations. There was no sentiment behind it. They hadn't cele-

brated Christmas like a family should since her mother
had been in the house.

Casting the maudlin thoughts aside, she returned
her attention to the reason she'd stopped by her sister's room.

She had an hour before her father, Patrick O'Malley,
returned from his Tuesday night board meeting. Sighing, she pulled the book off the bedside table. She
didn't know if Jo Anne had ever read *Pride and Preju-
dice* before, but it was one of Christy's favorite books.
Rather comforting on those evenings when she felt
melancholy. Or just tired. Like now. Ellie had not been
cooperative when she put her to bed. Lately, the five-
year-old balked whenever it was time to go to sleep.
No one did stubborn like her daughter.

Soon, she promised herself. Soon she'd leave this
poisonous environment and make a life for the two of
them elsewhere. Right now, however, she was shack-
led to this place by love and fear for the sister who had
protected her so many times.

She couldn't leave her only sister, who was helpless.

"Where did I leave off? Oh, yes, the ball at Neth-
erfield Hall."

She pulled her reading glasses off the top of her
head and perched them on the bridge of her nose. She
couldn't read a word without them.

"Tina."

Christy let out a thin shriek as a rusty voice from
the bed whispered the nickname only her sister and
mother had ever used. She leaped from her chair, the
book dropping to the floor as she hurried to the bedside. Jo Anne's eyes were open. Blurry and foggy with

pain, they zeroed in on Christy's face as she leaned over the bed, recognition shining in their depths.

A sob lodged in her throat, nearly blocking her ability to breathe her sister's name. "Jo Anne."

She couldn't say any more. It had been months since Jo Anne had spoken to her. Indeed, since she had last spoken with anyone. Jo Anne had defeated the cancer that had nearly killed her, only to be struck with an illness that plunged her into a deep vegetative state. Their father had brought her back to his house and set up a schedule of private nurses.

Everyone had been shocked. Patrick O'Malley rarely bothered himself with his daughters. When Christy had been a young child, he'd been a warm and devoted husband and father. However, all that had changed the night her mother had disappeared. He'd become indifferent, distant. Soon, his daughters had even begun to fear the stranger with their father's face. He'd never physically harmed either of them, but menace had cloaked him like a cloud.

"You should have left me." Jo Anne's hand fluttered weakly.

Blinking, Christy stared at her older sister's pale face, so much thinner than it was before she'd gotten sick. Leave her? How could she have left her like this? At the mercy of their cold, harsh father and his equally frosty second wife. Vanessa had never cared for either of the sisters, especially Jo Anne, who had enjoyed challenging her.

Christy's glance returned to her sister. Questions burned on her tongue, but she swallowed them. Now was not the time to ask Jo Anne about what had happened. There had been whispers of "overdose," but those whispers had always stopped whenever Christy had walked within earshot. She'd never believed it. However, the one person who had known the truth had been unable to talk.

Until now.

Scooting closer to her sister, Christy grabbed hold of Jo Anne's hand. It was painfully thin, fragile.

"I'd never leave you. You know that."

She was shocked at the strength in Jo Anne's grasp as she tried to pull herself up. Alarmed, Christy gently pushed on her shoulder to keep her in bed. "Hey! Hey, take it easy. I'm right here. I'm not going anywhere."

Jo Anne closed her eyes, but not before Christy saw the tears clouding her vision. One escaped and tracked down her cheek.

Christy gently wiped it away. "I'm here." She repeated herself several times, not knowing what else she could say to calm her agitated sister. When Jo Anne had settled a bit, Christy helped her to take a few sips of water and then settled back in her chair. She wasn't sure exactly what she expected to happen, but her instinct told her not to push or to move too fast. Jo Anne's mouth worked, and her eyes constantly bounced between the door and Christy.

Finally, Jo Anne sighed and her lids fluttered closed. Christy clenched her hands in her lap to hold back the thread of fear sliding through her. What if Jo Anne fell back to sleep? Would she have trouble waking again?

It was ridiculous to be so concerned, but these past months had been long and uncertain.

"So…tired," Jo Anne whispered. "You have to get out of here. It's not safe. I know too much, they'll kill me. Too weak to leave. You can't raise Ellie in this evil house." Her voice petered out again.

"Jo Anne, I think you might be confused. You've practically been in a coma for six months—"

Her sister's harsh, throaty growl stopped her as Jo Anne's eyes opened again, though it was obviously with effort. "I don't think they meant for me to go into a coma. I was supposed to die from an overdose." Her lids closed once more.

Christy remained in her chair, too weak to stand. She'd known that things were very wrong in this house. She'd been terrified of her father for her whole life. After her mother had disappeared when she was six, Christy had learned to hide in the shadows to protect herself. Her father had told her and Jo Anne that their mom had left them, but Christy had never believed it. How could a mother leave her children? Plus, she remembered the police officers coming to interview her father. Would they have done that if her mother had left of her own volition?

But still, for Jo Anne to be afraid of dying in her own house?

The door creaked open. Whirling, Christy stared at the doctor entering the room. He smiled at her, but the look in his eyes made her blood run cold. She blinked and the smile was gone. "Good evening, my dear. I need to check on your sister. Give us some privacy, please?"

Christy stood at the clear dismissal, but hesitated. It didn't feel right. Something about this whole situation was off. She desperately wanted to know what her sister had been talking about.

But how? She had no idea who Jo Anne thought

was trying to kill her. Was it all a dream brought on by her medications or her coma?

"Please ask Mrs. O'Malley to stop by." The doctor turned his back on Christy and walked around the bed to look at the IV.

Christy cast a single glance at her sister. Jo Anne was out. Unwilling to leave, but not really having a choice, she left and did as the doctor bade her.

Her stepmother wasn't pleased at the interruption, but snapped her laptop closed and marched off toward Jo Anne's room.

Slowly climbing the stairs once again, Christy passed by her sister's room and heard quieted voices inside. Knowing she couldn't return to Jo Anne's side now, she decided she'd stop by to check on her sister first thing in the morning. And find out what she had meant.

Five minutes after entering her room, Christy clambered into bed but found herself unable to sleep.

What "evil" had Jo Anne been talking about? Her insistence that someone wanted her dead scared Christy more than anything else. Could her ruthless father be that cold-blooded? She knew firsthand that he was meaner than a rattlesnake, but to try to kill his own daughter?

She thought of all the late-night business meetings as she was growing up when she'd been forbidden to come downstairs. Her father was an investment broker. Somehow, she didn't think all those people were meeting to talk about stock portfolios. She'd never trusted any of her father's guests, but she also couldn't imagine anything illegal happening inside his house.

If that were the case, she'd take Ellie and go. Although she had no idea where.

An outrageous idea started to form in her brain, but she pushed it aside. Ellie's father had no idea she even existed. Christy had been just shy of seventeen when she'd gotten pregnant. It had seemed so romantic, eloping with a boy not much older than herself. Looking back, she wasn't even sure they'd been really married. After all, both of them had lied and said they were eighteen.

It had been the happiest time of her life. Sam had made her laugh. Every smile had told her she was special and important to him. She would have done anything to be with him.

Until her father had found her in Shipshewana, Indiana. She and Sam were preparing to return to his home in Sutter Springs, Ohio, so she could meet his family. She'd refused to return home with her father, determined to stay with Sam. She'd given in when her father had threatened to have Sam arrested for rape if she didn't obey him. Sam had had his whole life ahead of him. She couldn't be selfish and let her father destroy him.

She'd done the only thing she could do and left. When she'd found out she was pregnant, she'd wanted to contact Sam, but knew it wasn't possible. By then, Jo Anne had become sick and needed her. By the time Jo Anne was better, Christy didn't know how to return to Sam to tell him he had a daughter. Until now, when he was her only option to protect their daughter.

Enough! She was letting her imagination run wild. Unable to sleep, she threw the covers off and slipped her feet into slippers. Walking past the window, she shivered as the wind howled and rattled the glass. Ice covered the panes. Christmas would be upon them in three weeks. Icy rain and sleet had been falling for the past six hours. The roads were one huge skating rink. Tonight would not be a good night for traveling.

She padded out into the hall. She'd make herself a cup of chamomile tea and honey to help herself relax, then she'd return to bed. She passed by the closed door to Jo Anne's room. Her steps slowed and finally halted.

Maybe she could just peek her head in to check on her sister. Surely there'd be no harm in that? Then she could pop down to the kitchen for her tea as planned.

Backtracking several steps, she tapped softly on the bedroom door and waited for the night nurse to respond. Nothing happened. Had the nurse not heard her? She had a sudden vision of the woman falling asleep on the job. It was probably nothing, but Christy couldn't stop unease from creeping through her veins.

She knocked again. Harder.

This time when no one answered, she pressed her lips together and turned the knob. The door swung open at her touch. Christy slipped inside the bedroom and pulled the door closed behind her. She stood in the dim light and blinked, waiting for her eyes to adjust.

The nurse's chair was empty.

That was odd. Jo Anne's nurse always stayed with her at night. She wasn't in the restroom. Christy had passed it in the hall. The door had been open.

Reaching out, she felt around with her hand until she touched the switch on the bedroom wall and flipped it. The overhead light blazed to life.

The nurse was indeed gone. Her coat and bag were missing, as well.

Christy glanced at the bed and the world tilted beneath her feet.

Jo Anne's eyes were wide open but there was no life in them.

Her sister was dead.

Grief held her frozen for three precious seconds before she became aware of quiet voices outside in the hall. She recognized one of them as Bryce's, the security guard. The other sounded strangely familiar, though she couldn't place it. Something in the tenor of their whispers had chills scurrying along her arms, making the hairs stand up.

Without stopping to think, Christy dashed inside the closet and closed the door, every instinct screaming at her to hide. She heard the bedroom door open. Blood pounded in her ears. Squeezing her eyes closed, she clasped her hands over her heart, breathing in deeply to stave off the panic attack clawing to break free.

"We'll have to close her eyes." Bryce's voice. "There's no bruising, so it doesn't look like she was smothered. We can say she died from the overdose."

"We shouldn't have to say anything. If you'd done your job right, she would have been dead months ago." The other man's voice was low, angry. "Simms said the other sister was in here earlier and might be suspicious. This one had started to talk, but we're not sure what was said."

"No need to worry about her. She's got a kid to protect. She'll not get nosy. Not if she knows what's good for her."

"Yeah. If the boss decides to put out a contract on her, I want to be first in line. I have a score to settle…"

Chilled by the reference to Ellie, Christy stopped listening. Jo Anne had been right—she couldn't stay here. Not if she wanted to protect her little girl. And what did he mean about a contract and a score to settle? What had she, or Jo Anne, ever done to anyone?

The horror was sinking into her soul. It sounded like a mob hit. Suddenly, the secret meetings made sense. Her father's business was a fraud. She'd had her doubts about it, but now she was sure. Something about his business had made his children targets. She didn't know who she could trust, not anymore. If Bryce was involved—a man she'd known all her life—well… who else was?

If Jo Anne had been a target, why had they let her linger? Now her beloved sister was gone, and her baby was in danger.

Grief spread through Christy like spilled wine on a cotton tablecloth. Soon, she'd be saturated with it and unable to think. She had to stay in control. Ellie was her priority.

The bedroom door closed. The men were gone. She needed to move.

It took all her will, but she stayed where she was another five minutes before venturing out of the closet and Jo Anne's room.

Christie approached the bedroom door slowly, setting each foot down as if she was walking on a fragile glass. She couldn't risk being heard. Placing her ear against the door, she listened, only opening it when she was sure there was no one in the hall.

Rushing into her room, she filled a backpack with a few necessities. Her phone was on the nightstand near her bed. She grabbed it and opened the settings. Quickly, she deactivated the location settings so she wouldn't have to worry about it pinging or alerting anyone to their whereabouts. She turned the phone off then shoved the device and a charger into the bag. She moved next door to Ellie's room. They had to escape in her car, but eventually she'd need to ditch it. She packed a little more for Ellie than she'd packed for herself, but not more than they could carry.

She'd taken long enough. Waking her daughter, Christy warned the child to stay quiet. Ellie's lower lip started to push out in a pout.

"We're going on an adventure, honey. I need you to not say a word."

At the word *adventure*, her big hazel eyes lit up and she nodded vigorously.

They snuck down the stairs and through the kitchen. Once outside, she loaded her daughter into her car. As she was backing out of the driveway, the side door to the house burst open and Bryce ran out, a huge man with a leather jacket and black beard beside him. She threw the car into Drive and gunned it as they yelled at her to stop.

Bryce lifted his arm. He had a gun! She pushed down on the gas as he fired. The blast shocked her. The bullet thudded into the passenger-side door.

Ellie screamed, but was uninjured.

Christy had little doubt the police would be searching for her car. She didn't know what story her father would tell them, but she knew she and Ellie were dead if they were returned to her father's house. A sincere face with the same brown eyes as Ellie's swam in her mind. Sam. She had to call Sam.

"Sam, you have a call." Adele grinned up at him. Sam Burkholder half turned his body on the ladder and raised an eyebrow at his cousin. "I have a phone call?"

Had he ever received a call before? As an Amish man, he'd grown up with no phone in his *haus*. The bed and breakfast his *onkel* ran had a phone, but only because it was a business that catered to *Englischers*.

He narrowed his gaze at his cousin. Adele had just turned eighteen and was readying for baptism into the church. She had a sparkling personality and tended to be somewhat of a prankster. Other than his family, no one would know to call him here. He didn't work at the Plain and Simple Bed and Breakfast. However, the roof had leaked earlier in the season and caused water damage that had needed to be repaired. Since his family owned a painting business, he was there on official business, prepping two of the upstairs rooms to be repainted. The job wasn't on the calendar, which meant he was running late to meet his *daed* and brother Abram at their next appointment. He should have left an hour ago.

He did not have time to play games with Adele today. "*Jah*, I am sure. I need to finish and move on. Take a message, will ya?"

"It's a *maidel*, Sam."

Her face was avid, burning with curiosity. Well, maybe she wasn't pulling his leg. He frowned. Other than his *mamm* or Adele, what females would be calling him? And they wouldn't call. He wasn't courting anyone. Hadn't for the past six years, although he could never tell his family the real reason why.

If they knew the truth behind his reluctance to go to singings or to meet any women, his *daed* would be sore disappointed in him.

He couldn't be more disappointed than Sam was in himself. He'd never be taken in again, even if he knew he was free to marry.

The problem was, he didn't know if he were free. And he had no way of finding out.

Aggravated, he shrugged. "*Ack.* I'm late. Adele, take a message. If it's important, I'll call back when I'm done."

She rolled her eyes and flounced off. Sam put the conversation from his mind and got back to his task. He had all but forgotten the incident until she returned ten minutes later. Her wide eyes and pale face told him something was wrong.

"Adele?" He hurried off the ladder. What had happened? Was someone hurt? Or sick?

She cleared her throat. "I gave her the message. She said she needed you to come and pick her up. I thought that was strange, and I tried to tell her you were busy. She said—she said—"

He tamped down his impatience. It wasn't often anything rattled Adele. "She said what?"

She sucked in a deep breath and released the words in a rush. "She said, 'Tell him his wife is calling.'"

Sam stepped back, his head reeling. His wife? There was only one woman who'd say that.

Looking around, he grabbed hold of Adele, pulled her onto the back porch and closed the door. No one could hear this conversation. "Tell me everything she said. Everything."

He hardly recognized that rasp as his voice.

She blinked. "It's true, then?"

He shrugged. "I don't know." He held up his hand before she could ask more. "It's a complicated situation, and one I need you to keep quiet about for now. Please, tell me what she said."

"She said she was your wife. She took a bus to Shipshewana, Indiana, where you met, and asked around until someone gave her this number. She said somebody was trying to kill her."

Christy never exaggerated. He remembered her, how much she wanted to tell the exact truth about everything. If she said someone was trying to kill her, they were. "Did she say her name?"

She shook her head. "She said she didn't want anyone to know who she was because they were searching for her."

It took him five seconds to decide he'd go. Even if she hadn't been in danger. He had six years of questions to ask her. Starting with, why'd she abandoned him? And why hadn't she let him know she was alive all these years?

"Okay. I need to find a driver. Shipshewana is a four-hour drive." He glanced at his watch. It was a little past nine now. Maybe he could get there before dinnertime. "I mean what I said, Adele. No one can know about this. If I'm not back tonight, you can tell anyone who asks that I went to assist a friend. No mention of who she is."

"Sam..."

He locked his gaze with hers. "I promise, I will explain everything to the family when I return home. But I don't have the time now. If Christy is in trouble, I need to go fast."

He waited until he had her nod of agreement then prepared for the journey, his stomach in knots. He'd fallen hard for Christy when they'd met six years ago.

So hard, he'd been tempted to leave his faith. He'd been carrying an emotional burden, one no one in his family had known about, and only Christy had seen behind his smile and calm demeanor.

He'd thought he'd found his forever love. Then she'd gone and his heart had broken.

Sam called around to find a driver. Finally, he found one. He had to wait nearly two hours for the driver to arrive, so it was almost six hours later when he stepped out of the car and asked the driver to wait for him. He wiped his hands on his trousers. Regardless of the snow and ice surrounding them, he was cold. He wasn't sure he had the right place, but she'd said to come where they'd met. Buses lined the parking lot.

Where to begin searching?

He went inside and scoured the depot with his eyes. In the back, nearly hidden, a woman squatted next to the wall, a small girl beside her with her little arms crossed as a storm brewed on her face. She was about five seconds shy of a temper tantrum.

Sam stared at the terrified woman in front of him. She was six years older than the last time he'd seen her, but he'd know her anywhere. Even with her head turned away, he'd memorized the curve of her jaw. Her face was slimmer, more mature, but he knew her.

"Christy?"

Her dark brown eyes shot to his when she heard her name, widening as she took in his appearance, from his heavy black boots, simple trousers and winter coat, to the hat pushed down on his head. She'd never seen him dressed in his Amish clothes. When they'd met, he'd been going through a defiant phase.

"Sam?" Her voice trembled, although whether

it was shock, fear or a combination of the two, he couldn't say.

"Mommy, I'm scared."

He glanced at the child snuggled up against her side. Then his eyes widened. The child looked exactly like his cousin Adele had when she was little. Right down to the huge hazel eyes gazing at him with suspicion.

"Christy." He never took his eyes from the munchkin as he addressed the woman. "Who is this?"

"This is my daughter. Eleanor Samantha. I call her Ellie."

Samantha. Could be a coincidence. He didn't believe in coincidences. Forcing his stare away from the child, he read the truth in Christy's face. Not only was the girl he'd loved back, but she'd also had his child and never told him.

"I can explain," she said, her words rushed in the awkward silence. "But I need your help. Someone murdered my sister last night, and they're after us. If they find me, they'll murder Ellie and me, too."

TWO

Sam took a step back, mentally shaken by her revelation. Her sister had been murdered?

"I never knew you had a sister." He realized that he had known very little about the girl he'd loved enough six years ago to go through with a forbidden wedding ceremony. All he'd known was that she had a harsh, demanding father and a spoiled stepmother. He hadn't even asked about her biological mother's whereabouts. Had she died? Had Christy's parents divorced? Why hadn't he ever asked these questions? Had he really known her?

"I know you didn't," she whispered. "There were many things we never told each other."

Jah, that was true. They'd been together for such a brief time. He'd told her some things about his family. Just not everything. He remembered literally running into her at the bus station when he traveled to Shipshewana during his *rumspringa*. Her vibrant personality and bright smile had attracted him from the moment they'd collided. Sam had taken a summer job in Shipshewana to put some space between himself and Sutter

Springs. They'd been inseparable for two short months before they'd decided to get married.

Sam had planned on bringing her home to meet his family, even though he was still at war with himself about his part in what had happened to his brother, who had left the Amish and become *Englisch* for a few years. Levi was back now, but he'd been through a lot.

Levi had left after an argument with his father because someone had accused Levi of theft. How much of his brother's suffering could have been averted had Sam done the right thing? Sam had never told his father, or Levi, that he'd known who the real thief was. He'd thought he was helping his best friend. In fact, he'd thought his best friend would come through for him and do the honorable thing. But he hadn't.

The little girl at Christy's side began to fuss.

Nee, he corrected himself. His daughter. While her hair was the same rich color of dark molasses as her mother's, rather than light brown like his, the curls that fell to her shoulders were all his. Christy's hair fell past her shoulders in a straight sheet without a single wave. Eleanor—or Ellie, as Christy had called her— also had his hazel eyes rather than Christy's warm dark brown color.

"Why didn't you tell me?" His throat constricted as he strove to control his emotions.

She sighed. "I wanted to. Believe me. If I had thought it was safe, I would have."

Safe? "I don't understand."

"I know you don't. But now is not the time. Sam, I drove my car here. It's sure to be recognized. Please. I don't know if the police will believe my story, or if I'll even have the chance to tell it."

The fear in her eyes decided him. He had made some bad decisions in his life, a handful concerning the woman in front of him. He should never have consented to that wedding ceremony, no matter how in love they were. Even though she'd expressed interest in joining the Amish church, he had known at the time it wasn't the right thing to do. Wrong or not, however, they had married. And she'd raised his daughter herself. She claimed she had done it to protect him.

Could he believe her? She'd abandoned him once, and she'd never told him why. He wanted to believe she was being up-front with him now, but he found it difficult to trust so easily. Not to mention the difficulties this would make for him at home.

Well, he couldn't take the chance. If they were in harm's way, he had to act. It was his duty. And he'd never forgive himself if something happened to them.

"Okay. I can wait for an explanation." He dropped his gaze to Ellie. "She looks tired."

"And hungry."

Ellie nodded emphatically. "I'm hungry, Mommy. My tummy hurts, I'm so hungry."

He wanted to wipe the anguish from Christy's face. *Don't be fooled, Sam.* He'd never let himself fall into the trap of love again. People tended to abandon those they loved far too effortlessly. *Nee,* he was better off steering clear of that emotion.

But he couldn't ignore the sweet little *maidel* looking at him with such hopeful eyes.

"There's got to be a vending machine or a little restaurant around here." He planted his hands on his hips as he looked around him. "Let's see if we can find Ellie something to eat."

Ellie's tiny hand slipped into his. "I'm hungry, mister."

He grinned down at her, his heart melting into a puddle. That didn't take much, he scoffed silently as his eyes snagged Christy's. How did they tell her who he was?

"Honey, this man isn't just 'mister.' He's your daddy."

Daed. He bit back the correction. His daughter was being raised in the *Englisch* world. Whether he liked it or not, that wasn't likely to change.

Instead of the warm welcome he might have hoped for, Ellie drew back, her face blanking in an instant. Whatever reaction he'd expected, it hadn't been that. The child appeared almost frightened of him.

"He's not like my daddy, Ellie." Christy's broken whisper reached his ears. "He'll protect you and love you."

The little girl's lower lip trembled. "Will he yell a lot?"

"Nee." It was time he entered this conversation. No child should be afraid of their father. "No, Ellie. I will not yell a lot. I promise."

Sam took one of the backpacks from Christy. She held Ellie's hand and the small family went in search of something to eat. In the end, they found a small stand that sold sandwiches. Christy and Ellie waited at an empty table while Sam purchased the food.

Ellie gobbled down a tuna sandwich like she was starving. Christy, he noticed, barely nibbled on hers.

"You okay?"

She nodded, sliding a glance at Ellie. "I don't like staying in one place for so long. I keep expecting someone to find us."

"Christy, what happened?"

She dropped her gaze and took another nibble. Stalling, no doubt. He didn't want to upset her, but it was time he had some answers.

"Yesterday?" She still didn't raise her eyes.

"*Jah*, yesterday, but also six years ago." He gestured toward their daughter. "You left—"

"I didn't leave." Her eyes snapped to his face. "Not willingly."

He raised his eyebrows. "Explain, please."

"I'd run away from home and taken a bus and got off here. I didn't plan on sticking around. When I met you, I changed my mind. I never dreamed I'd be traced so easily. My father had found me. I had gone to the mall to get some new shoes, remember? When I got back to my car, he was there waiting for me. He had hired a private investigator who'd found me. My father forced me to go with him. I wanted to return to you, especially when I knew…" She gestured at Ellie.

He nodded; yes, he understood.

"By then, though, my older sister had been diagnosed with cancer. Jo Anne had no one to stand with her as she went through treatments."

"She would have had your father, right?"

Christy snorted. "My father was never one to be comforting. I think he found her illness an inconvenience. And my stepmother had never been fond of either of us. I couldn't leave her alone."

He remembered that about her. Christy had always had a keen sense of compassion. He recalled how outraged she would become when she read newspaper articles about people suffering or being mistreated. He knew her well enough to understand that she wouldn't have been able to leave her sister alone. But still…

what about him? Their marriage? Shouldn't her devotion have extended to him? At the very least, couldn't they have talked about her options? There was more she wasn't saying. He was sure there was.

But perhaps she was right. Now was not the time.

"I'll accept that for now."

Relief crossed her face. "You'll help us?"

"*Jah.* It will be awkward for me, but I will help."

Her forehead creased. "What do you mean? How will it be awkward?"

"I don't live in Shipshewana, as you obviously remember, since you called my *onkel*'s bed and breakfast. I live in Sutter Springs, right outside of Berlin, Ohio. That's where my family is from. My family that has no idea what happened when I was seventeen on my *rumspringa*."

She blinked at him. "You mean they don't…"

He faced her squarely. "I waited to hear from you, so we could tell them together. When you never returned, I went home to Sutter Springs. I never mentioned you. My family can't understand why I never attended singings or never showed any interest in setting up *haus* with anyone. They don't know that I might be married."

Christy processed what he was telling her. His family had no idea that he was married. Well, she couldn't blame him. She hadn't told her family much, either. Mostly because she was scared of what her father would do to Sam. Maybe things would have been different if Jo Anne hadn't been dealing with the effects of chemotherapy. But by the time her sister had been declared cancer free, several years had passed and Christy didn't know how to approach Sam with the news that he was a father, although he'd told her enough about his family that she knew where to start looking for him.

She paused as his exact wording caught her attention. "Wait. What do you mean 'might be married'? You went through the same ceremony I did."

Yet hadn't she been wondering earlier if their wedding had been valid?

"You don't have your doubts? We were both barely seventeen. While we can marry younger in an Amish community, neither of us had parental consent. Plus, you know we both said we were eighteen."

She sighed. "True. But the guy officiating never asked for proof of our age."

"Christy, he never asked for any kind of identification at all."

"That's why we chose him." She shrugged. "It was the only way we could do it without needing our parents' approval."

He laughed, but there was no humor in it. "Which should make us both wary. What kind of official doesn't ask for documentation?"

"You're right. And, if I'm honest, I've had doubts, as well."

He ran a hand over his chin. "I'm afraid that I might get into a lot of trouble when my bishop finds out. First, that I went through with the ceremony to someone who wasn't Amish, and then that I never said anything."

Christy winced. She certainly didn't want to cause trouble for him. She didn't know enough about his culture to know what to expect from his family. Or what they would expect from her. At one time, she'd been planning on joining his church, but that seemed like a ridiculous idea now. Who joined the Amish church just to escape her overbearing father?

It wasn't that, though. At least, not only her father. She'd truly believed they were in love and that love could overcome anything.

She'd been so naive. Love had failed at the very first test.

She frowned. "When we met, I knew you were Amish, but you weren't always dressed like you are now."

Ellie's food was gone. Christy began gathering up the garbage. Sam took it from her and tossed it in the trash can before picking up the backpacks again. They began walking.

"This is my everyday look." Sam grinned and gestured to himself, picking up the conversation again.

He sobered quickly. "When we met, I was trying to decide if I still wanted to be Amish. There'd been some trouble in my family a few years before I met you. My brother Levi left us, and we didn't know if he was alive or dead. I was angry at him for abandoning us. And I was mad at my *daed* for the argument that forced him to leave." He shook his head. "Mostly, I was mad at myself. *Daed* was accusing him of something— of stealing—and I knew Levi hadn't done it. I didn't come forward in time. By the time I told my *daed* what I knew, Levi had gone."

Her heart constricted. Poor Sam! Then she blinked, remembering what he'd said. "And then you thought I'd abandoned you, too."

It was like shutters closing over his eyes. His whole face lost expression as he gave her a single nod.

Even though she'd told him her father had forced her to return home, he still felt she had left him. And, given she hadn't contacted him, she couldn't argue. She had chosen her family over him, even if she hadn't wanted to.

It was better that way. Because, by the looks of it, he'd chosen to stick with his Amish life. That was good for him. She didn't know much about the Amish lifestyle, but she did know that if he left the Amish church, he'd also be leaving his family and his home, which he loved. She couldn't do that. But she no longer had any desire to become Amish, either. Besides, her family was bad news. It would only bring Sam trouble if they got back together. She would rely on him only as long as she needed to, to figure out where she and Ellie could go to be safe from her family.

She remembered the man in her sister's bedroom talking about a contract and a score to settle. With her family? With her? She hadn't recognized him. Why had he sounded so familiar? If only there was someone she could go to who might have the answers. Her father was out of the question, obviously.

Reaching into her bag, she brought out her cell phone. "I think I should do a quick check to see if anyone has reported us missing."

Turning on the phone, she brought up her browser. A quick search showed no new information. "I don't see anything. Maybe we're good, for now."

Sighing, she turned the phone off. She had no way to know when she'd be able to charge it. She needed to preserve the battery. Unfortunately, the phone had given her something else to focus on. Once it was put away, there was only Sam and Ellie. And the horrible situation she was trying to escape.

Sam, despite his misgivings and hurt feelings, was willing to help. Somewhere beneath the bitterness, she sensed the boy she'd loved was still there. But getting close to anyone, even the man she considered to be her husband and the father of her child, could only spell danger. For her and Ellie, and for him.

No, it was better if he held on to his anger. He'd come out of this alive and wouldn't search for them when she disappeared. Again.

She squinted as they exited the dim bus depot and walked into the parking lot. The afternoon sun struck the snow, creating a blinding glare. Her eyes watered at the brightness. Instinctively, she turned toward her car.

"Nee." Sam grabbed her arm, letting go when she paused. "They'll look for your car, ain't so? I have a driver. He's over there, waiting for me."

Her eyes followed his pointing finger to the dark SUV waiting near the back of the parking lot. The driver waved at her.

"Okay. Yes, they'll look for my car. I need to grab Ellie's booster seat out of the back."

"Give me your keys."

She handed them over without thinking. He jogged to her car, his long legs carrying him much faster in his sturdy boots than her fancy wedged-heeled footwear would allow her to walk. She flushed, feeling foolish in her fashionable but unsuitable attire.

"Come on, Ellie. We're going to go in Daddy's car." She probably shouldn't encourage the child to think of him as her father. But he was. She couldn't deny it, not now that they both knew it.

By the time they arrived at the SUV, Sam had the booster seat in place in the back. "You and Ellie can get in."

They both climbed inside and he shut the door behind them.

She turned to say something to Sam, who was in the front passenger seat.

"Get down!" he ordered a second before she saw the flashing strobes of the two police cars that had roared into the lot and positioned themselves to block in her car.

Her heart stopped. They'd have to drive past her car to leave the lot.

She pulled Ellie out of her seat and into the well of the floorboard.

"Mommy!" The little girl started to cry.

"Shush, honey. It's fine. Mommy just needs you to be quiet for a few minutes. We don't want your grandpa to find us."

The little girl's tears dried immediately. "Will Daddy save us from Grandpa?"

The fear in her voice broke Christy's heart. No child should fear their relatives. It was wrong on every level.

"I'm going to do my best, Ellie."

From the floor, she peered up him. She'd never seen him angry before, not like he was now. When he turned and stared out the window at the cops, she understood. He wasn't mad at her. No, right now all his anger was directed at the man who'd put terror in the heart of his daughter. For that moment, she knew he was on their side.

THREE

"Let's go," Sam told his driver, keeping his voice low. Ellie was scared enough already. "But slowly. I don't want them looking this way. Christy, you and Ellie need to stay down until I say it's all clear."

He didn't glance her way to see her response, afraid it might seem suspicious if someone saw him looking in the back seat. The whispers and the rustling behind him told him she was following his instructions. His neck ached from the tension.

"I don't know about this, man," Mike, the driver, whined, a distinct fret in his voice. "I ain't never been in trouble with the law. I don't want no part of anything illegal."

Sam turned his gaze on the man. He was young. Maybe in his late twenties, just a few years older than Sam, and had a shiny wedding ring on his hand. Newly married? He'd never hired Mike to drive him before, so he didn't know that much about him. Mike had no reason to trust him, either. What if the man decided to turn them over? Sam needed to persuade Mike to help them, or it was all over.

He smiled to put the man more at ease. "*Nee*, nothing illegal. My wife and my daughter are in danger. I know it sounds unbelievable, but we need to get away from here."

The driver flicked his glance up to the rearview mirror, probably to catch a glimpse of the two passengers hunkered down in the back seat. "Your wife? She doesn't look Amish."

"I was planning on becoming Amish." Christy's voice whispered from behind him.

Was planning on becoming Amish? The bitterness seared Sam's aching heart. Just today, she'd admitted that she didn't know much about the Amish, yet she'd planned, once upon a time, to join them. Why would she want to join a faith she didn't understand? Becoming Amish wasn't like joining a club. Had she been using him to escape her family when they'd first met?

How could he ever trust in her love? He almost snorted when he recalled that, mere hours ago, he'd reassured himself of her honesty. Now, he wondered if he ever really knew her.

Apparently not. Nor had she known him.

Yet she'd called him when she'd found herself in trouble. No matter what she had done, or her reasons for doing it, he was a father now. The little girl shivering in the back seat deserved his protection. Briefly, he closed his eyes and prayed for guidance. Only *Gott* knew the whole truth. Sam had to believe that He would be with them and help them.

Mike put the car in Drive and started to pull out. Sam glanced around as they drove slowly from the parking lot. When Mike braked at the stop sign and put on his blinker, Sam gritted his teeth. Mike sat at the stop sign for an absurdly exaggerated amount of time before slowly pulling out and onto the road.

At least it felt that way to Sam.

"It's best to make sure you're stopped completely if you don't want to get pulled over for ignoring a traffic sign," Mike explained when he met Sam's eyes. Still driving slowly, he left the lot and headed east. When they had gone about a mile in complete silence, Mike finally spoke up. "I don't want to do anything illegal. But that kid's scared of her peepaw. Anyone who'd scare a kid that much is not a good person."

"Understood." Sam looked around him. "I don't see any police cars. Christy, you and Ellie can get into your seats. Buckle up. We have a four-hour drive to Sutter Springs."

Christy and Ellie scrambled out of their hiding space. He watched them in the mirror on his visor.

"So, we'll get there after dark?" Christy buckled Ellie into the booster seat. The belt clicked into place and then she tickled the little girl under her chin. Ellie giggled and hiked her shoulders up, pinning Christy's hand in place. A smile forced its way onto Sam's face. He couldn't help himself. Ellie's giggle was a ray of sunshine in what had become a disturbing and dark day.

Sam turned his head and watched as Christy buckled herself in. Her face was pale, but he still thought she was the prettiest woman he'd ever met. He shook his head. Where had that thought come from? Physical beauty was unimportant. Her eyes met his, stormy and sad. She had courage, he'd give her that.

What had she asked? "*Jah*, we'll get there late."

She hesitated and bit her lip.

He waited. When she didn't continue, he shrugged. Then he realized she knew nothing about where they were going. Or his family.

"My brother Levi and his wife, Lilah, live about ten minutes from us. My other brother, Abram, recently married. We built them a *haus* nearby. That leaves just me in the *haus* with my *mamm* and *daed*. Tomorrow, we'll go see Bishop Hershberger. He'll need to know everything that's happened."

He didn't like the fear that entered her eyes.

"You'll be fine. Don't worry about him."

Those glorious brown eyes narrowed. "That's not what I meant."

His eyes widened at the irritation in her voice.

"I'm not worried about me." A sigh left her. She reached a hand up to massage the back of her neck. "I'm worried about you. How will your bishop react to you having a wife and a five-year-old daughter?"

He'd wondered that himself, but it warmed him to know that she was concerned for him.

"There's no use wasting energy on being anxious, ain't so?" He shrugged and infused his voice with false confidence. "We can't know how he'll react."

"You act calm, but I know you, Sam. You've always been good at burying what you're really feeling deep inside. I bet you're feeling just as nervous as I am."

He blinked, startled by the observation.

Beside him, Mike snorted. "Dude, I think she's going to win this argument."

He'd forgotten about their audience. Flushing, Sam turned his face toward the window.

He squirmed mentally in his seat for a moment. In the end, he had to admit she was right. He did tend to hide what he was feeling. Hadn't he done that with Levi? And with *Daed*?

Apparently, Christy knew him better than he'd thought she did. Not that it mattered. He couldn't allow himself to relax his guard around her.

All he knew was that if you let people see into you too much, they were able to use you. They could hurt you. He had learned that lesson when his best friend Martin had let Levi take the fall for stealing money from Martin's *daed*.

He would never let himself be that weak again. Not for a friend. Not for anyone. Not even for a woman who might be his wife.

A wife that he would never be able to accept. She wasn't Amish, and he wasn't the insecure teen once willing to let go of his faith.

They were at an impasse.

She couldn't see his face anymore, but Christy knew Sam was disturbed. Or angry. Maybe both.

She couldn't blame him. She'd never considered what kinds of problems her showing up suddenly might cause for him. But she'd been out of options and the people coming after her would have no compunction about using Ellie.

They'd had no problem killing Jo Anne. Briefly, she wondered what story her father and his cronies had given to the police to make them come after her?

"Sam, we need to know why the police are searching for me." She blurted the words without thinking, immediately wishing she could call them back. Now was neither the time nor the place for this discussion.

In the front seat, Sam shifted so he was looking at her again. "What are you thinking?"

She shook her head, flicking her glance to Mike then back to Sam. "Just thinking out loud. How long until we get there?"

He tilted his head and gave her an expression that plainly said *Please*.

Clearly, he knew she was dodging his question. Still, he let the subject drop. "We still have three and a half hours, miss," Mike called from the front seat, clearly not catching the heavy tension hanging in the air. "You'll be late for dinner. It's not snowing, though, so that's a plus."

She leaned her head back against the seat and closed her eyes.

"Christy? Are you okay?"

She grimaced. "Fine, Sam. Just tired."

So tired. Exhausted, really. She was totally adrift with a young child, being chased by killers, and her only hope was a man who didn't trust her and had every reason to be a bit hostile toward her.

Yeah. She was just peachy.

The urge to sob herself into oblivion hit her hard, but she managed to swallow the lump swelling in her throat. She would not give in to tears and display her weakness. It was imperative that she remain strong for Ellie.

"Watch out!" Sam shouted.

Christy's eyes shot open and she spun in her seat to look around her. A truck was roaring up behind them. It was a huge beast of a pickup.

"Why doesn't he go over to the other lane?" she grumbled. The passing lane was clear. Traffic on the US 30 was light. It wasn't a road that was typically clogged with traffic.

"Because he's not trying to pass us," Sam said, grabbing the handle next to the window as Mike hit the gas. "He's trying to run us off the road."

"Mommy!" Ellie shrieked, beginning to cry as the SUV continued to increase its speed. "Don't want to go this fast! I'm scared, Mommy. Make him slow down."

"Sorry, kid," Mike muttered. "I don't like going this fast, either."

Christy comforted the child, craning her head to look at the dashboard. They were going eighty-two miles an hour! The speed limit was probably fifty-five or sixty. She couldn't look away as the numbers continued to climb.

Slam!

Jolted, her head whipped forward, though her safety belt caught her and pulled her back against the seat.

"He hit us!" Christy screamed.

"Christy! Ellie!" Sam called out, swooping his head around to check on them.

"We're okay!"

"Hold on!" Mike yelled, jerking his wheel to the left as a vehicle tried to turn onto the highway.

She made the mistake of looking out the window. The truck was moving into the other lane.

Her breath caught as the black-bearded man in the leather jacket leaned out the passenger-side window of the beastly pickup. He seemed to struggle for a moment, then he pulled a rifle out.

"Sam!" she yelled, her hands already unbuckling herself and Ellie and dragging them back down to the floorboard.

Mike tried to evade the truck and the gun targeting the SUV. The rear window shattered among Ellie's terrified shrieks. Glass rained down upon them. Christy drew her daughter to her, curving her body around the child.

There was a second shot.

The SUV started to spiral out of control.

"He got the tire!" Mike shouted. "I can't stop it!"

Between the blown-out wheel and the incredible speed, the vehicle slid and spun across the road. She felt it knock against something, but it didn't stop.

"Mike! There's a car!" Sam's voice rang out seconds before the collision.

The air was filled with a sharp whoosh as the front airbags deployed. Sam groaned and the vehicle creaked as it rocked to a stop.

A siren split the air. Police? Or an ambulance?

Mike hissed. "Man, that hurts."

Wondering if the man in the leather jacket would come to finish them off, Christy quickly checked Ellie over for injuries. She didn't see any. Wiping the tears from her daughter's soft cheeks, she kissed her and hugged her close, more grateful than she'd ever been.

"Sam?"

"*Jah*, I'm well."

He sounded out of breath. Had he been hurt and refused to say?

"Look," Mike said, interrupting her thoughts. "That guy took off. He obviously doesn't want the cops to find him. But he was going to kill all of us. You guys, go. Get out of here. Try to get home and see if you can stay alive."

"You sure?" Sam was already opening his door.

"Yeah. Anyone who'd target a kid can't be trusted. I don't care if the law is on his side."

When Sam opened her door, she saw what had happened. They'd collided with a guardrail. There was a second vehicle in the ditch. The pickup was nowhere to be found. Scurrying out of the SUV, she stood on legs that shook in delayed reaction.

Sam reached past her and grabbed the booster seat. She opened her mouth to ask what he was doing, then shut it. There was no time.

"Mike would have to explain where it came from." Sam slammed the door. "We'll ditch it as we go. Button your coats."

She fastened the top button of her jacket and adjusted Ellie's hat. Taking her daughter's hand, she grabbed the backpacks and led Ellie after Sam as he walked away from the SUV and onto the side street intersecting US 30. She had no idea where they were.

It was freezing cold. It would soon be dark. And they had killers after them. When Ellie stumbled and whimpered, Sam held the booster seat in his left hand, then reached down and picked up the child in his right, holding her close. Ellie put her head down on his shoulder.

"Let's keep moving," Sam murmured. "We have a long way to go."

Christy reached out and touched her daughter's shoulder before nodding and following Sam's lead. She prayed with all her heart that her father's men wouldn't locate them. Deep inside, she had trouble believing that her father would willingly kill her. He was cold and distant, but he was still her father.

But he hadn't saved Jo Anne. Had her sister been killed on his order? And if Christy came face-to-face with her father now, would she and Ellie make it out alive?

FOUR

Sam ditched the car seat within twenty minutes. When Ellie started to squirm, he set her back on her feet. Christy held her hand as they stumbled after Sam. Her boots had not been made for walking through the snow—that was for sure. The pretty little wedged heels were anything but practical. Since they came only to her ankle, it wasn't long before her feet were wet, cold and aching.

Fortunately, she'd been smarter and less vain when it came to her daughter. Ellie was wearing dirty winter boots, the kind perfect for children to run and romp in the snow for hours. Her short legs, however, soon grew weary after trouncing through eight inches of snow-covered ground and her cheeks were red from being buffeted by icy winds and the occasional snow squall.

"Mommy, my face is cold." Ellie sniffled, her nose red and running from the chill.

Christy stopped and leaned down. Ellie's scarf was damp, both from the falling snow melting into it and the water vapor caused by her breaths. She unwrapped the garment and stuffed it into a side pocket on the backpack. "It's a good thing I grabbed two scarves."

She pressed a soft kiss to Ellie's cheek, both to show her affection and to gauge the temperature of her skin. It was cold, but she didn't think it was dangerously so. The wind had died down, and the temperature was hovering around thirty. She wrapped the second scarf gently around her daughter, taking care to not rub the knitted fabric against the chapped skin.

"Is that better, sweetie?"

Ellie nodded, her head bobbing up and down in exaggerated movements. "Uh-huh. But I'm tired. I don't want to walk anymore. I want to go inside and play with my dolly."

"Your dolly's in your bag, sweet pea. I know this is hard, but I need you to be my big girl now and walk, okay?" Christy's heart was crumbling inside her chest. Her poor baby girl. There was nothing else she could have done, she knew that. If she had stayed, they might both be dead by now.

Dead. Like Jo Anne. Her sister's lifeless gaze swam before her eyes. She blinked back the emotion blurring her vision. She didn't have time to dwell on the horror of the past twenty-four hours. She had too many other things to deal with right now. Like staying alive and not freezing.

"Christy? Are you all right?"

She stood and faced Sam, taking Ellie's small hand again. "I am." She glanced down at her daughter. When she met his eyes again, she kept her voice to a whisper. "I'm struggling to keep my head above water, to not get bogged down with memories."

He searched her face then nodded. "*Jah*, I understand. We need to keep moving. We're not safe."

That Sam included himself in their situation

warmed her clean through to her wounded soul. He didn't have to help. He hadn't known about Ellie until now, and he had more than enough reason not to trust Christy ever again. But he hadn't abandoned them. In fact, he'd joined their quest so readily that she knew it was a statement of his character, that he would never abandon his family.

Not like she'd done to him.

She hadn't thought she'd had a choice, at the time. Could she have defied her father, though?

No. She couldn't have risked it.

Stop. None of this matters. Not anymore.

Sam picked up Ellie's other hand then reached over and plucked the backpack from Christy's shoulder. Surprised, she gawked at him for a moment before she blinked and started to protest.

"I can carry it, Sam. I don't expect you to carry both."

He shrugged but didn't hand either of the bags over to her. They plodded farther away from the road they'd left behind, each step fraught with resistance due to the snow buildup.

"I know you can. But now you don't have to." He didn't glance her way as he urged Ellie to take another step.

He was good with children. Ellie was tired and cranky, but she followed his instructions. When she whined, he didn't show any sign of impatience or irritation.

That's what a father looked like.

"Tell me about your family." Sam's voice was low and casual. Almost as if he was asking about the weather or something immaterial. It was a facade for Ellie's sake.

"It's not a fun story." Christy shoved a branch out of the way so it wouldn't smack her in the face. "My mom disappeared when I was around Ellie's age."

"Disappeared?" His left eyebrow vanished under his dark bangs.

She nodded. "Yes, disappeared. My dad insisted she left us, but I can't believe that."

For three heartbeats she let the silence fill the space between them.

"My dad…he changed after she left." She bit her lip, unsure how to explain.

"Jah?"

"Yeah. Before she left, I have vague memories of my dad teaching Jo Anne and me how to ride our bikes, taking walks to get ice cream, and reading stories together. Sometimes he made up stories to make us laugh. Afterward, though, the laughter was gone. When he married Vanessa…" She shook her head. Grief settled on her shoulders like a heavy cloak, weighing her down.

"Christy?"

She cleared her throat. "He met her at some kind of work event. I remember him coming home and asking me if I'd heard of Vanessa McCormick. I thought it was strange. She seemed to know about our family. I met her and wasn't impressed. She was… I don't know. I guess *aloof* is the word. I didn't even realize they were dating at first. They married quickly, without warning. And just like that, my dad was this cold stranger. All of a sudden, Jo Anne and I were prisoners in our own house. We couldn't go anywhere without his knowledge. When he had meetings at night, which had never happened before, we had to be upstairs in our rooms."

"I didn't like it there, Mommy." Ellie interrupted their conversation. "Grandpa was mean and Mrs. O'Malley didn't like me."

Christy shifted her eyes toward Sam's. She had hoped her daughter hadn't been listening to their conversation.

"'Mrs. O'Malley'?" Sam's jaw dropped. "Christy, is she referring to your father's wife?"

The red flooding her cheeks had nothing to do with the chilly temperature. She dropped her gaze, unable to meet his any longer. It was mortifying, seeing her family through his eyes. Sam's family, she was sure, was a far cry from the dysfunction she had been raising her child—their child—in.

"Yes." How much should she say? Well, he needed to know, and Ellie had figured things out on her own. Still, she couldn't bring herself to be as blunt as she wanted to be. A parent had to protect their offspring, even if it seemed a lost cause. "Vanessa says she's too young to be anyone's grandmother, and she hates the term 'stepmother.' Too Cinderella-ish."

Even if the term seemed appropriate.

Sam snorted then coughed, looking ashamed.

She laughed. "Don't worry about offending me," she chided. "I'm the one talking trash about her."

A soft sob broke from Ellie. The smiles dropped from both their faces as they looked down at the child. "My hands are cold. And wet. And I'm tired." The complaint litany was accompanied by another sob.

Sam bent to remove her gloves. "Your hands are ice cold. Here, Ellie, let me help you."

Removing his own gloves, he stuffed her little hands into them. He slid the two backpacks from his shoulders and held them out to Christy. Wordlessly, she took them. Sam reached down and gathered their daughter into his arms again. The child snuggled into her father's shoulder and within moments was asleep.

They continued walking.

"Why did you stay with Ellie in that place?"

She couldn't blame him for the censure. "I didn't want to, but I couldn't leave Jo Anne. And my father was paranoid about security. We were always watched. I'm amazed that I managed to get away the night my sister was killed. If everyone hadn't been so involved with her, I don't think I would have been able to pull it off."

"I'm glad you did." He started walking. "If what you say is true, you might not have gotten another chance."

Sam didn't believe in coincidences. Christy had apparently lived under her father's thumb for years. Given the constraints, it seemed highly unlikely that she would have been able to escape the same night her sister was murdered. If anything, he would have expected the strictures that had been upon her for years to have tightened. How had she managed to escape? She'd been followed and shot at, and still was here with him, unharmed.

This was no coincidence. With all his heart, he believed *Gott* had stepped in to shelter her and help her out of a very bad situation.

"I think you had *Gott* on your side."

His words broke into the silence with the abruptness of a gunshot.

"God?" A world of disbelief coated her velvet tone.

His heart sank. "*Jah, Gott.* You are here and safe. You don't agree?"

He remembered her blossoming faith six years earlier. Had that faith been smothered by the darkness that had surrounded her?

"I don't know what to believe anymore, Sam." She ran a hand lightly over Ellie's back, as if to reassure herself that the little one was all right. "When we were together, your faith was so appealing. The way you talked about God. Even though I suspected your faith had taken a beating, I never understood why."

It was true. He'd let his anger and his guilt over what had happened with his brother and his *daed* make him doubt *Gott.*

"I had some struggles, *jah*, but I have put them aside."

Struggles he didn't really want to go into now. His heart still ached when he dwelled upon all that Levi had suffered because of his silence. If he had been braver, or if he had not trusted the wrong person, it could have all been avoided.

He was too gullible at times. Right now, he was in as much danger of falling under Christy's charm as he had been when they were seventeen. A single glance from her was like an arrow of warmth that sank into his heart. It was imperative that he take care. He couldn't afford to lose his heart to her a second time. He had an idea of why she'd left him before. The bonds of family were strong, and he knew what it felt like to have a sibling in trouble. However, even if they didn't

have a history, the truth was he was Amish. He had
joined the church, and was determined to follow the
rules of the *Ordnung*. With *Gott*'s help, he would stay
true until the day *Gott* called him from this earth.

Christy, on the other hand, had made no such com-
mitment. She might have planned to at one time, but it
was now clear those ambitions were gone.

The only connection between them was Ellie.

He would never abandon his *kind*. Although, he had
no idea how to go about being a father to a *kind* whose
mother lived in the *Englisch* world.

"It's going to be getting dark in a couple of hours."
He pointed to the sky. The sun had begun its descent,
creating long shadows in its wake. "We should try to
find food and some shelter before the night sets in."

"It's supposed to go down into the teens tonight."
Christy pulled Ellie's hat down. Her knuckle grazed
his chin, leaving a trail of warmth where she touched
him. She jerked her hand back, flushing, and averted
her brown eyes.

"We need to step up the pace."

He tightened his grip on his daughter and trod east,
forcing his mind away from the brief contact. It was
hard to believe a simple touch from Christy could still
affect him this way. He hardened his heart. No matter
how beautiful she was, no matter how smart or how
tender she treated their child, Christina O'Malley was
nothing but trouble.

If only he could convince his heart to remember
that.

A strained silence enveloped them. It was broken
only by the crunch of snow beneath their feet and the
occasional hum of distant road traffic. The sounds of

its flow became more frequent and much louder as they continued to walk.

"Shouldn't we be reaching a town soon?" Christy stumbled over a root buried under the snow. He reached out one arm, careful not to disturb their daughter, and steadied her. Even that brief contact threatened to disturb his equilibrium.

"We should be coming upon something soon," he remarked. "We've been walking for almost two hours."

Ellie began to stir in his arms. His heart thawed a little more at the way she snuggled and sniffled while waking up. Rubbing her nose with her sleeve, she sat back. Her sleepy gaze swiftly changed. He saw the storm coming and rotated his body so she could see Christy keeping pace with them. "Don't worry, Ellie. Your mother is here. See?"

Ellie stretched out her arms to her mother. Gently, he set her down and she flung herself at Christy.

"Here, let me take the bags."

She gladly handed them over then enfolded Ellie in a hug. "It's okay, sweet pea. We're still walking. You fell asleep for a while."

The quiet they'd enjoyed was a thing of the past. Ellie, adorable as she was, was keen on making her complaints known.

"I'm hungry!"

"Soon, Ellie," Christy promised.

"I'm cold, too." The little girl folded her arms across her chest and thrust out her bottom lip.

"Walking will keep you warm, ain't so?" Sam offered a hand to her, attempting to coax her to keep going.

Having none of it, she turned her face away from

him. "I don't want to walk. I want to eat, and I don't want to be in the snow anymore."

"Here. Let me have the blue backpack again." Christy dug around inside the bag and found several protein bars at the bottom. Ellie scrunched up her nose, but apparently was too hungry to refuse them.

Once they'd eaten, Sam announced they should continue on their way.

It took some coaxing, but the child reluctantly allowed them each to hold her hand and lead her along. The evening was getting darker and colder by the minute as the sun steadily descended below the horizon. Hues of orange, pink and purple bled out across the landscape.

"What a fantastic view," Christy murmured. "I'd enjoy it so much more if—" She broke off.

Sam understood. "*Jah*, if."

If they were safe.

If they were somewhere inside.

If killers weren't hunting them down.

FIVE

Christy couldn't remember a time when she'd ever been so cold. Or so bone-tired. They had been walking for hours, and her feet were numb. So were her hands within her thin gloves, her cheeks, her nose. She didn't know if she would ever be able to get warm again.

She said nothing out loud. Not only would it do no good, but she didn't want to set her daughter off again. Ellie had finally agreed to move with them, and Christy didn't want to encourage yet another tantrum.

Poor kid. Ellie had really been a trooper during this whole adventure. It was a lot to ask of a five-year-old. Unfortunately, the way things were going, she'd be asked for a lot more.

Just as Christy reached the point where she didn't think she could go another twenty steps, Sam called her name.

"Look!" he said, pointing up ahead to the left.

At the sight of a small house half-hidden by the trees, her heart began to race.

"Oh! I hope someone is home. Maybe they'll be willing to help us." Even as she said this, part of her was amazed. Just a short time ago, she would never have entertained the idea of knocking on a stranger's door to ask for assistance. Yet now she was blinking back tears at the sight of a little house in the distance.

With renewed optimism, the trio marched toward the house. As they neared it, however, some of that hope drained from her heart. It didn't take long before she realized her hopes and wishes were going to go unanswered.

The house was abandoned. Shingles had fallen from the roof, and the shutters clung loosely to the windows, ready to drop if a stiff wind hit them at the right angle. The porch steps were badly in need of repair.

There would be no one inside to assist them. No phones. No electricity.

"There's a woodshed." Sam touched her arm. He pointed at the small ramshackle shed cozied up next to the cabin. "The *haus* might not be much, but there's wood stacked in there. The cabin might not be perfect, but I can probably get a fire going. We can get warm, and get rested up, and start out fresh tomorrow morning."

It wasn't what she wanted, but it was better than continuing to trudge through the snow. She nodded.

Five minutes later, they climbed the steps and Sam stepped forward to push open the door. The hinges creaked in protest as it slid open.

At least no bats flew out of the house, but she kept that observation to herself. There might not have been bats, but that didn't rule out all sorts of critters that could have holed up in the little cabin for the winter. A shudder ran down her spine as she considered the possibilities.

Christy was a city girl through and through. She

did not relish the idea of sleeping in the same house with rodents. There was no choice, though. The lure of warmth was stronger than the fear of any wildlife they might find in the house.

Pasting a brave smile on her face, she skirted a spot where the porch had rotted through and crossed the threshold, bringing Ellie with her. Ellie, rather than clinging in distaste, was wide-eyed with wonder. Her mouth formed an O as she turned in a circle, looking around the dark cabin like it was a palace, instead of a small space reeking of mold and things that Christy had no desire to know about.

It was awful.

"Well, this isn't so bad, *jah*?" Sam stepped in behind them and glanced around with satisfaction. He almost looked happy.

Was he serious, or was he acting for the sake of Ellie?

She had a sinking feeling that he was not playing.

"Daddy, it's like a hidden treehouse, or a secret cave. Maybe there are dragons or monsters in the closets!" Ellie was bouncing in her excitement.

"Dragons and monsters would be a good thing?" Christy asked, raising her eyebrows.

Sam chuckled and moved farther into the room. When he looked up the chimney, his smile grew. "*Gut.* No bats or nests in there."

Christy shuddered. He laughed at her expression but headed outside. She peeked out the door and saw that he was heading to the woodshed.

"Okay, sweet pea. Daddy is going to make a fire so we can get warm. Let's see if we can find anything to sleep on."

She glanced briefly in the cupboards. There was no electricity, but she was able to lay her hands on a variety of candles and some matches. They would have to do for light. She lit a few and placed them strategically around the open living room and kitchen area. Standing in the center of the room, she sniffed and wrinkled her nose.

Sam entered the cabin with his arms full of firewood. He kicked the door closed behind him, crossed the room and dumped the wood in front of the fireplace. He started to squat but halted halfway down and frowned.

"Why does it smell like a flower shop in here?"

She laughed. It came out like a strangled cough. "I found some candles for light. Unfortunately, they're all scented. And not a single duplicate." It was a bit overpowering.

She coughed again.

He rose. "That can't be *gut* for your asthma."

She waved a hand. "I have my inhaler. As soon as you have a good fire going, I should be able to put the candles out in this room. It's for one night."

He stared at her for a moment. "If you have trouble breathing, we'll put them out. A little light is not worth making you ill or uncomfortable."

She wanted to protest but didn't. First, it meant a lot to her that he had remembered her asthma. She'd never had an attack in front of him and had only mentioned it a time or two that she could recall. Also, he was right. If she had an asthma attack, it would be more serious now because they were literally in the middle of nowhere with no electricity or a way to get to the hospital. She had her phone, but she would prefer not to drain the battery. If she had to call 9-1-1, she would have to keep the phone on until help arrived.

And if help arrived, would the doctors at the hospital call her dad, thinking next of kin should be notified?

She didn't even have a wedding certificate to prove that Sam was her husband. Nor did she have any proof of insurance.

She had nothing.

Whatever she could do to avoid going to the hospital, she'd do. She nodded at Sam. "I'll be careful. I promise. I won't take any unnecessary risks."

He stared a moment longer then nodded, turning back to his task. She let out the breath she'd been holding. His eyes, those deep hazel wells, still had the power to make her forget what she was doing. Realizing she was standing there watching the muscles play across his shoulders, she blushed and scurried to the closet, hoping to find some blankets that would keep Ellie warm that night.

It took a while for the house to warm up enough for them to remove their coats. Upstairs, she found two small bedrooms and a small closet that had been converted into a bathroom. The rooms were so cold, her breath misted in front of her face. Even with the fire Sam had built, the rooms upstairs wouldn't be warm enough to sleep in at night, not with the electric heat turned off. She'd have to create makeshift beds in the living room for each of them. It was probably better that way. They wouldn't have as far to run if escape became necessary.

Moving downstairs again, she sighed in pleasure as the warmth from the fireplace washed over her. As long as they stayed away from the outer walls and windows, the draft wasn't too bad. Christy found some still-edible canned goods in the cupboard. Nothing fancy. A can of green beans, some baked beans, some tuna and a can of pears. It was a strange mix of foods, but by the time it was dark, they were warm, and their stomachs had stopped aching with hunger.

Ellie started to droop in her seat at the table. There were no chairs, just a couple of hardwood benches. As she started to slump, Sam stood, gathered her in his arms, and moved to the center of the room. Christy, having found some blankets in the closet, told him she'd been surprised to find so much as she joined him at the makeshift mattress.

"My guess is this was a summer home. Still might be, seeing how some of the food is so recent and there are so many items here. Also, I'd have expected to find the *haus* infested if it had been empty long. As it is, I'd say this place has been empty maybe a few months."

"It looked a little rough on the outside."

He smiled. "*Jah.* They probably had a bad storm or two in the off season. The inside, as you can tell, was kept up fairly well."

She nodded. It made sense. "I'm glad we found it. It would have been a long night if we hadn't."

Sam lay Ellie down on the pile of bedding Christy had set up in the center of the living room area. She had it arranged so that she would sleep on one side of Ellie and Sam on the other. She wanted her daughter to be safe, to know she wasn't alone if she woke in the middle of the night.

She should warn Sam. "Just so you know, Ellie sleepwalks sometimes when she is feeling extra stressed. At my father's house, I had a baby monitor I would use to wake me if she moved."

He nodded. "I used to walk in my sleep as a *kind*."

Her eyes widened. That was news to her.

He stacked the wood in the fireplace and closed the screen. "That should burn through the night. Do you have your phone on you?"

"Yeah. It's off to save the battery. Why?"

"I was wondering if you could do a map search to find out where we are and maybe where we should head in the morning. You know, so we're not wandering blindly."

"Oh! Great idea. Hold on." She pulled the device from the bag and pushed the button to turn it on. When the light flashed and it chimed loudly, she cringed, praying Ellie wouldn't stir. A quick glance confirmed that the little girl had slept through it. Christy drummed her fingers on her thigh while waiting for the phone to finish starting up.

"Finally." She unlocked the screen and swiped her finger up, finding the map app. When it opened, she and Sam sat together at the table for a few minutes, discussing which direction they would head in the morning. Sitting beside him, his warmth sizzled through her, making her stomach quiver. She ignored it, although she couldn't stop the flush from crawling up her neck.

"It looks like we're only two miles from a town." He rubbed his chin thoughtfully. "We could eat breakfast then hike in that direction. It should only take an hour or so."

"With a five-year-old?"

She wasn't as optimistic as he was.

"Maybe two hours."

She rolled her eyes and turned the phone off. "However long it takes us, we'll be better off if we get a few hours of sleep. I hope I'm wrong, but I doubt I'll sleep very soundly tonight knowing there are killers out there searching for us."

Sam lay awake long after Christy drifted off into an uneasy slumber. He could tell by the way she mumbled and tossed and turned that she wasn't having pleasant dreams. It was to be expected. At one point, she'd been so restless, he'd almost reached across Ellie's sleeping body to shake Christy awake to rescue her from whatever tormented her.

She seemed to calm a bit before he could carry out the intervention, so he'd let her sleep. She needed it. So did he.

He sighed. His parents must be worried about him. Adele would have let them know that he was heading into Indiana. How much had she told them? He grimaced and flopped over onto his back. His muscles protested at the uncomfortable roughshod bed, but he'd never complain. Christy had used what was available, and she and Ellie were sleeping on the same things.

His thoughts returned to his family. His *mamm* and *daed* were bound to be disappointed in him once they learned of Christy and Ellie. They wouldn't refuse to help them. They were far too generous for that. But to marry outside of the Amish church? Well, that wasn't something one did. His one saving grace would be the fact that he hadn't been baptized at the time of the marriage. In fact, his parents had believed for a short while that he had left the church. His bishop, however,

might not agree. Sam hadn't been Amish, true, but
he also hadn't confessed everything he'd done when
he'd returned. Closing his eyes, he fought the thoughts
clouding his mind so he could rest.

Sam sat up, the blanket covering him slipping to
his waist. The fire had burned down to little more
than coals in the bottom of the fireplace, with an occasional snap and crackle. The light from the blaze
had also diminished to a hazy glow. Other than that,
the room was dark.

What had awakened him?

Beside him, he could hear the quiet breathing of
Ellie and Christy. They were both safe.

The sense that something was wrong didn't leave
him. Quietly, he shoved his blanket off and slipped his
boots on his feet. He moved around the *haus*, checking the upstairs rooms and the bathroom. They were
all empty. He noticed the broken window in the bedroom on the left. Walking over to inspect it, he saw
that it looked out over the roof. He opened it. There
was no screen. Animals would be able to get in if it
was left open.

He started to shut the window then stopped.

The distinct sound of motors hummed on the night
breeze.

ATV motors, if he was hearing correctly. And they
were close. Too close.

Even as he listened, the engines hummed closer. He
could see the lights coming as the machines turned up
the lane to the *haus*.

They'd been found.

He didn't know how he knew this. Maybe he was

paranoid and it was just some kids out goofing off. He'd rather not take the chance. They were almost here, whoever *they* were.

Leaving the window open, he rushed down the stairs, leaping over the bottom step in his haste to waken his daughter and his wife. He didn't even pause to consider that he'd thought of her as his wife.

"Christy!" He gave her shoulder a shake. She bounced up with a gasp before he could give her another shake.

"Sam?"

"I think they've found us. ATVs are coming up the lane."

She was already scrambling into her boots and coat and grabbing Ellie's clothes from in front of the fireplace. Their daughter protested being jostled so abruptly, but a whispered warning from her mother had her awake and silent. Her face grew still as her big hazel eyes filled with fear. At her look, he felt as if someone had reached inside his chest, grabbed his heart and squeezed it.

The engines were roaring up to the front of the cabin.

"How will we get out?" Christy breathed, swinging the backpacks onto her shoulders. He finished getting Ellie in her boots and swung her up into his arms. The child buried her face in his shoulder and grabbed his neck in a choke hold. "We'll have to go out another way."

"Another way? There's no back door." Her whisper rose with desperation.

"*Cumme.* Follow me."

He hurried over to the steps and led her up to

the room he'd vacated earlier. The blast of cold air slammed their faces as they entered, shocking any remaining sleep from them, as if the adrenaline weren't enough.

He let Ellie slide to the ground when he reached the window so he could climb out first to test the strength of the roof. He bounced on the balls of his feet a couple of times. It felt sturdy enough. There wasn't any noticeable give in the surface.

"Wait." Christy stared at him through the window. "Sam, what are we doing?"

"Shh. Keep your voice down." He gestured for Ellie to step up to the window then proceeded to help her out. When she was standing next to him, he motioned to Christy. "*Cumme.* It's the only way."

The ATV engines were idling in front of the *haus.* He could hear low voices. They were not the tones of kids. These voices, low enough that he couldn't make out the words, were deep and rough. The voices of angry adult men.

"It's the only way, Christy. We have to jump."

She stared at him as if he'd spoken in an unfamiliar language, her mouth falling open. "Jump?"

"*Jah.* We can't go out the front door. This is it."

As if to emphasize his point, the sounds of boots on the front porch startled her into a tense silence. She nodded and climbed out onto the roof.

Sam waited to make sure they were standing securely before moving carefully to the edge. He looked over. The tree beside the roof wouldn't be hard to climb, but he doubted Ellie could tackle it.

"I'll go down the tree first."

"I'll lower Ellie to you."

Now that they were ready to implement his plan, he decided it was awful. There was no other option, but he wasn't happy with this one. He made a quick jump and caught the tree branch closest to the roof. He nearly lost his grip.

"Careful!" Christy demanded in a strident whisper.

He got a better grip and scampered down the tree. Once his feet were firmly on the snow-covered ground, he reached up and beckoned for her to lower Ellie to him.

To his surprise, Ellie didn't appear to have any of the fear or worry her parents were feeling. Instead, she let her mother lower her toward her father. When her feet were in front of his face, he nodded at Christy and she let go.

Ellie fell into his outstretched arms with a *whomp!* He hugged her briefly and then set her down at his side. "It's your *mamm*'s turn."

They both looked up at Christy. She tossed the backpacks down then turned and lowered herself over the edge.

Sam caught her feet and steadied her. "Now!"

When she dropped, he wasn't prepared for the impulse to hold her close as she slid against him.

The urge faded as they watched flashlights flicker inside the *haus*. Motioning for Christy and Ellie to follow him, they crept along the exterior of the *haus*. At one point, they heard the voices from inside the *haus*.

"Are you sure this is the place?"

"They were tracked here."

"Well, they ain't here anymore. Obviously, they were here recently. They can't have gone far. Let's check upstairs before we report in."

The faint sound of boots clomping up the stairs spurred Sam to push Ellie and Christy toward the front of the *haus*.

The ATVs were there, waiting for their owners. Sam smiled. How nice of the men to leave them a get-away ride. He set his jaw. It had been a long time since he'd driven an ATV. He hoped they hadn't changed too much.

A brief thought about whether he was breaking the law flittered through his mind, but he swatted it away. He knew what he had to do.

Christy and Ellie pressed up against him, their warmth infusing him with determination to do whatever he needed to do to survive. He recalled a conversation he'd once witnessed between his brother Levi and his wife, Lilah. She had been relieved that Levi hadn't gotten in trouble for driving a truck when they'd been in a literal life-and-death situation.

Levi had shrugged. "When your buggy goes into a ditch, you use whatever means you can to pull it out."

Sam felt Ellie take his hand. Christy's breath was warm on his neck. These two were his to protect.

This was a buggy-in-a-ditch situation if ever he'd seen one.

SIX

Sam kept close to the *haus* so as not to be seen by the two men prowling around inside it. The two were making no attempt to be silent, believing that the occupants had already fled. The sun was just beginning to peek over the horizon, which meant he didn't have much time before they'd be visible in the morning light.

Christy scooted closer and leaned against him to whisper. Her breath on his ear nearly distracted him from what she was saying.

"What are we doing? Shouldn't we be running toward the road?"

He shook his head. "They'll come after us. If we take the ATVs, we can make better time. We can leave the four-wheelers somewhere on the side of the road. It'll be harder for those two to catch us on foot."

She sucked in her breath at his plan. "That's audacious."

He grinned in the darkness at the note of surprise in her voice. "Can you ride one of those things?"

"Yeah. Can you?"

"Jah."

The ATVs were still running. Probably not very

energy efficient, but Sam was grateful that the men intent on hunting Ellie and Christy had been in such a hurry that they'd left the keys in. Praying to remain undetected, he climbed on the one nearest to the front door. Reaching out, he picked up Ellie and settled her on the seat with him. If they were discovered, he'd rather they shot at him. He'd make a bigger target, and his daughter would be hidden by his bulk.

Seconds later, leather creaked as Christy settled onto the other ATV. The rising early-morning light chased shadows over her face, obscuring her features from him. He remembered her posture more than he'd expected to. Grim determination emanated from every line of her slim body as she gripped the handles of the ATV.

She nodded at him. He reciprocated. In sync, they put the vehicles in gear and the engines roared to life. It had been a while since he'd driven one of these and, for a brief moment, it looked like it wasn't going to move.

But as the ATV jerked forward, there was a shout from behind him. Instinct had him turning in time to see one of the men holding a gun at the ready. Sam sped up at the same time the gun blasted behind him.

Ellie screamed.

"Sam!" Christy half turned in her seat.

"I'm *gut*!" He hugged his daughter to him. "Go! Go!"

They tore down the lane and across the white landscape, allowing the shouts and gunshots behind them to fade. He'd been so intent on escaping, he'd paid no heed to the direction they were traveling. Sam looked over his shoulder and blinked at the rising sun. He shot his arm up to shield his eyes against the glare coming from behind him.

He halted the ATV and honked at Christy. She glanced back and halted, too.

"Daddy, why are we stopping?" Ellie peered up at him, her little face avid and flushed. So, his daughter liked excitement, did she? He grinned at her, but his face straightened as Christy dismounted and ran back to his side.

"What is it? What's wrong?" Her attention shifted to Ellie. She examined her daughter for any hint of injury or harm.

"*Nee*, nothing is wrong with Ellie. Christy, she's *gut*." He waited until he had her attention.

"Then what is it?" She frowned up at him. This time, he noticed she was checking him out. He bit back a smile. The situation was anything but amusing. Still, he found her concern moved him.

"The sun is behind us." At her blank look, he pointed at the sun climbing the horizon. "Sutter Springs is east. We should be riding toward the sun, not away from it."

A glimmer of despair flashed briefly across her lovely face and vanished. No doubt, she'd gotten so used to putting on a happy face for Ellie's sake that she did so automatically now. His heart ached that she'd needed to learn such a skill.

"Which means we need to turn and head east." She said it as if it was no big deal.

"It's not that simple." He ran his hand over his chin as he considered their plan. "Those men are sure to be looking for us. We had planned on dumping these

ATVs at some point. I would suggest now would be the time."

She sighed. "That means we'll have to hoof it from here."

He chuckled at the term. "*Jah.* We go on foot. We need to use back roads as much as possible."

Her expression brightened. "There is one benefit. If we dump these here, when they find them, they'll think we headed west, so maybe they'll continue traveling west."

He shrugged. "Maybe so. But let's not stand around talking. We need to move."

It took only a few minutes to gather their belongings and an exuberant Ellie. Now that she was rested and had had a morning adventure, the child was chipper and talking faster than anyone he'd ever heard. It was hard not to laugh at her enthusiasm.

Christy, he could see, was less eager to head out on foot again. "Remind me never to wear fashionable boots when I'm going on the run, will you?"

He shot a glance at her feet. Although attractive, her boots were highly impractical. While the heels weren't that high, the boots were obviously not made for any sort of hiking or distance walking.

"I'll be sure to remind you. It might not be a bad idea to buy you something more weatherproof when we have the chance."

She rolled her eyes. "Ya think?"

"Let's take the keys with us so they can't use these to chase us down," Sam said.

They pocketed the keys and took off as quickly as they could with Ellie.

Whenever they heard an engine heading their way,

the trio ducked off the road. Even though they weren't on the main roads, there was always the chance someone would be searching for them along the less popular routes. Sometimes they found themselves sitting in a ditch or behind a tree.

After the third time, Sam started feeling a bit foolish ducking out of sight. "Do you think they've given up?"

Christy scowled. "Not likely. These are men who have much to lose. Remember, they've murdered Jo Anne, and they have to think I either saw them or suspected. Especially since they chased us and shot at us. No, we're still in danger. My father won't let us go this easy."

He couldn't even process a father wanting to harm his *kinder*.

Another engine hummed along the road, heading toward them from the east. Without a word, they both grabbed one of Ellie's hands and nearly flew back behind a line of bushes along the roadside.

By this point, Ellie knew better than to complain, although her expressions grew more and more turbulent each time they made a dive for cover.

The vehicle came over the hill. It was a plain, ordinary SUV. One Sam would have never given a second glance. Beside him, however, Christy gasped as a second car hummed along from the opposite direction. Instead of passing, as he'd expected, both vehicles slowed. The driver-side windows slid open.

"Did you find them?" a male voice ground out from inside the car.

"No, sir." This voice, coming from behind the wheel of the SUV, sounded older. It was still one of the coldest voices he'd ever heard. Sam had no trouble believing the man behind the voice would be capable of killing.

His hands landed on Christy's and Ellie's shoulders. He wanted them to know he was there. That he would keep them safe, no matter the cost. He couldn't make out the faces of the men. Frustrated, he listened.

His jaw hurt. He'd been grinding his teeth.

"Do another loop. They can't have gotten far. The ATVs were still warm." The man inside the car started to raise the window but stopped as a third voice complained from inside the SUV.

"It don't feel right. I don't hold with hurting kids."

Sam's muscles went taut. Beside him, Christy started to shake. He slid his hands off their shoulders and pulled them both close against his sides.

"It doesn't matter what you want to do, Kip. You're paid to do a job—unless you find this work doesn't suit you. In that case, we'd have no use for you."

Kip got the message. He stammered out an agreement.

Both drivers rolled up their windows and went on their way. To an observer who couldn't hear them, it might have looked like one had stopped to get directions. Who would believe they'd been so calmly discussing a hit on a woman and a child?

Wetness hit his hand. Christy was crying, silent tears falling down her pale cheeks. He had no words to comfort her.

"Christy, we'll make it." He knew better than to promise such a thing, but he couldn't hold the words back in the light of her distress.

"It's not that." She sniffed and wiped her damp

cheeks with her sleeve. "I recognized the man driving the car. I can't be sure, but I think he's the doctor who treated Jo Anne. I'm pretty sure he's the one who killed my sister."

Sam looked like someone had knocked the air out of him. Christy knew that feeling well. That's how she'd been feeling for the past two days. Longer, if she were honest with herself. Ever since her sister had gone from being in remission on one day and she'd found her lying in a coma the next. Drugs... Overdose... She'd heard the whispers. The lies. She had known, with the soul-deep certainty of a sister who adored her older sibling, that Jo Anne had never touched drugs.

That man—the one in the car—he'd been the doctor who had visited that night. Simms. That's the name Bryce had said.

"Simms," she murmured. She caught Sam's questioning glance. "I heard Bryce, one of the men who'd chased us, refer to a man named Simms. It might have been him. He was pretending to be a doctor. I can't prove he's the one who killed Jo Anne, but he was definitely in the know."

"We need to get out of the open. The sooner we make it to my home, the safer you'll be." Sam's words were decisive.

Her stomach knotted. How much danger would her presence put his family in? Sam looked at the sky.

"We'll keep heading east. There's nothing else we can do."

Her nerves jangled around inside her as they walked. Not knowing what was coming for her, or why these evil things were happening, had stripped her of her peace of mind. To distract herself, she peppered Sam with questions about his lifestyle.

He was reticent at first. And why not? The questions she was asking could have been overly personal. Soon, however, he began to open up and tell her about his family.

"Levi, he's the one who left us for a time, he was a soldier."

Her jaw dropped. "Isn't that forbidden?"

"*Jah.* But he wasn't Amish anymore. He lost an arm saving a fellow soldier. When he returned, he was a changed man. He's married now. His wife, Lilah, is a fine woman. They have a couple of *kinder*. He's a deacon in the church now. Abram, my other brother, lives close by, too. He married his childhood sweetheart last year."

He continued to speak about the *Ordnung*, or the rule that his family lived by, the simplicity of their lives.

She'd had no such simplicity in her life. Vanessa was very conscious of their wealth and how the outside world perceived the family. Her father went along with whatever she demanded. That had often put him at odds with the wishes of his daughters, but they had learned it was better not to argue.

She shook her head to chase the thoughts away.

"Sam, I don't know. Your family...will they mind helping us?"

"*Nee.* You are in danger. They will help."

In the end, it was Ellie's tired face that decided her to stop arguing. They needed to get to a safe place. Her little girl was her biggest priority.

"Mommy, Daddy. My tummy hurts. I'm so hungry." Ellie's complaints broke through her thoughts.

Sam hunkered down in front of their daughter, his gaze tender as he looked into her mournful face. A lump formed in Christy's throat. If only she'd been able to stay with him, they could have raised Ellie together.

Although, that would have meant becoming Amish. Honestly, after living for so many years under her father's rule, she didn't know if she could have abided following even more rules.

"*Jah*, I know you are, Ellie. As soon as we can, we'll stop and find something for you to eat, okay?"

They walked for another twenty-five minutes, Ellie whining more with each progressive moment. When they reached the outskirts of a small town, Christy was ready to cry with relief.

"Christy, you and Ellie hide out here. I will go in and buy us some food. I doubt anyone would recognize me."

"Okay." She watched him walk away. She didn't want him to leave them, but he was right. It was quite possible that she had been reported missing. Or worse. She shivered, recalling the cruisers at the parking lot at the bus station the day before. Was that only yesterday? It was hard to believe, but she knew it was Thursday, only two days since Jo Anne's death and the ensuing rush to escape her father's henchmen.

"Daddy's coming!"

It was clear by the way Ellie whispered that she sensed the gravity of their current circumstances. Christy winced. No child should have that kind of knowledge or experience. Her duty as a parent was to shield and protect her child. How she had failed!

Glancing up, she gasped. Sam was dashing across the street like he was on fire. What had happened?

Sam crashed to a stop before them.

"Why were you running?" She clenched her hands to control their trembling.

"Stay back." He cast a quick look across his shoulder, scanning the horizon. She leaned over slightly to peer around him. No one was coming. When he relaxed, she slumped back against the wall.

"I saw someone come into the store," he said, handing Ellie a boxed pizza. Her eyes glinted with delight. They watched while she opened the box and scooped up a slice oozing with cheese and tomato sauce. She bit into it, ginning with pleasure. Christy pressed her lips together to hold in the chuckle when her daughter looked up, sauce on the end of her nose.

"You saw someone?" She prodded him to continue once it was clear Ellie was completely diverted by the pizza.

"*Jah.* I can't be sure. There was very little light at the *haus*, but I thought it was one of the men who were there."

She reared up, ready to flee in an instant.

"Relax, Christy. He got into a car as I was leaving. He's gone."

"But they were there." How had they found them?

"We need to get away from here, fast."

"I agree. But let's think about how we plan to do this. It's a hard walk. The trip from Shipshewana to Sutter Springs is four hours in a car. Walking, we'll be heading that way for days in freezing temperatures and snow. Before I saw one of our bad guys, I looked at the weather forecast in one of the newspapers on the rack. It's going to be fifteen degrees tonight. Fifteen."

She was cold just thinking about it. And what about Ellie? Her breath hitched in her throat, nearly choking her. Temperatures that cold were too brutal for grown adults to handle. A small child would have no chance for survival.

"Sam." She had to clear her throat so her words wouldn't come out garbled by the fear that was clenching her. "What can we do? I don't have any family or friends nearby who can help us. Anyone I can think of might give our position away."

It was horrible realizing that people she'd known most of her life couldn't be trusted. Then again, very few people suspected her father was capable of the heinous things he had done. Even she had her doubts, and she lived in the same house with him. She'd never actually seen him do anything evil. But the suspicions had been brewing for years.

"We have to find a ride." He shrugged his shoulders as if to say it was no big deal.

It was a huge deal.

"Hitchhike?" Her throat was strained from trying to keep her voice modulated. "Do you know how dangerous it is to hitchhike?"

He quirked his eyebrows. His mouth twisted. If sarcasm had a face, that was it. "More dangerous than being chased by mobsters?"

He had a point.

Christy pulled in a deep breath. This went against every instinct. But she had to protect her daughter.

"Okay. I'm not sure this is a good idea, but you're right. We're out of options."

He nodded and bowed his head. "*Gott*, please help us get to safety."

She blinked at him when he raised his head and started to walk toward the street. When was the last time she'd heard someone pray so openly, without embarrassment? Never. Faith had truly never been a part of her life. Even when she'd thought of joining the Amish, it had been about Sam and leaving her father. God hadn't been on her mind at all. And even though he'd talked about his faith, Sam hadn't been one to pray out loud in front of others.

She was seeing a side of Sam she hadn't known existed.

While Sam flagged down a ride, she took Ellie into a Dollar General to use the restroom. She arranged their hair to cover more of their faces. It wasn't much of a disguise, but it was the best she could do. Maybe she should've waited for Sam, but if the store manager recognized her later, she didn't want him to remember that she was with an Amish man.

When they returned, Sam had begged a ride from a woman named Elaine driving an SUV. Christy thanked her, then she, Ellie and Sam piled into the back seat of the vehicle. Her teenage son made no bones about gawking at them. Apparently, he wasn't used to his mom picking up strangers. He looked about thirteen or fourteen and was wearing a junior high wrestling team hoodie.

"I won't be able to take you too far." The woman's eyes met hers in the rearview mirror. "Ben and I are on our way to an overnight wrestling tournament. We have to be there at a certain time for weigh-ins, or he won't be able to wrestle tomorrow. Otherwise, I'd take you farther."

"We understand," Sam responded. "It's a long way to my home."

Briefly, Christy wondered what story he had told the woman. She had to be wondering why they were on foot with the five-year-old. Then again, she had to be wondering why he was traveling with them anyway. She frowned. They'd draw less attention if they were all dressed the same way. At the moment, that seemed unlikely.

Elaine drove for an hour, randomly chatting with Sam and Christy, every now and then making a comment to her son, Ben. As for the teenager, he rarely answered with more than a monosyllabic grunt.

It was midafternoon by the time she pulled into a hotel parking lot. "This is where we'll be staying. I need to check in and then we need to head over to the arena to get him weighed in."

"I wonder if they have any available rooms," Christy murmured. She caught Sam's questioning gaze. Using her chin to point, she called his attention to their daughter. Ellie had fallen asleep. "She's exhausted."

His mouth drew down at the corners. He didn't like it—that was clear.

He opened the door and stepped out of the SUV, then he reached in, unbuckled their daughter and gently lifted her into his arms. The little girl murmured in her sleep, but didn't waken. Instead, she nestled closer. He stood for a moment as if thinking.

After thanking Elaine for the ride, neither of them

said anything more until Elaine and her son had gone inside the hotel to check in.

"I know you're right," he said, "and I don't want to stop. But we've traveled forty miles from where we were. We'll have to be careful and we have to leave first thing in the morning. I don't have any credit cards on me."

She nodded in agreement. Digging into her bag, she pulled out some money she'd grabbed from her room before leaving the house. "I hope this is enough. They might be able to trace credit cards."

Sam jogged inside. Fifteen minutes later, just when she was thinking she should risk it and find him, he returned. "I got two rooms. They're connected."

"That's fine."

They didn't talk as they walked to their rooms.

She had never appreciated a shower and a bed more. They were able to order food from the diner across the street. The hotel wasn't huge, so there weren't that many people to bump into. Most of them seemed to be wrestlers and their families.

"Stay in the room until we leave." Sam's voice was low, even though they were using the connected door in their rooms. Ellie was already curled up in the double bed, snoring lightly.

"We will."

He hesitated. "We should also leave this door unlocked."

Her eyes widened, but she didn't argue. "You're right. Although…"

She had no words to express the horror she felt at the possibility of needing to escape again. He reached up and tucked a strand of hair behind her ears. His hand brushed her cheek then dropped. She could have almost imagined it.

Almost.

Without a word, he ducked into his room and closed the door, separating them. She leaned her back against the door and crossed her arms over her stomach, hugging herself to quell the trembling. She hated feeling so vulnerable.

Forcing herself to step away from the door, she moved toward the bed and then stopped. She wasn't afraid of the dark, never had been. Tonight, however, the idea of not being able to see anything freaked her out and sent needles of panic down her spine.

She flipped on the bathroom light then quietly sank onto the edge of the bed, careful not to wake her daughter. Pajamas would have been more comfortable, but she made do with sleeping in her clothes, again. Inching over, she held her daughter close as she closed her eyes. It was hard to relax, even in the comfortable surroundings.

The danger wasn't past. Even with this short respite, she knew those searching for them wouldn't let up until they were brought to justice. Or until she, Ellie and Sam were all silenced. Permanently.

SEVEN

Sam stood on the other side of the door for a full five minutes before he could convince himself to move. Every muscle in his body was tense, willing him to rush back into the other room and stay there to protect his daughter and the woman he considered his wife.

It wouldn't be proper.

It had been one thing when there was nothing else to do. When they had fallen asleep in the cabin, there'd been nowhere else for him to go where he wouldn't freeze to death. Here, he had his own room.

A man did not sleep in the same room with a woman. And even though he'd gone through a wedding ceremony with Christy, he knew he could not consider her his wife. Not only because of the circumstances in which they'd been wed, but also because of where their separate lives had taken them.

Even if he had no doubt as to whether or not they were married, he still would be forced to treat her as if they were not husband and wife. Christina O'Malley was out of his league. She had gone back to her *Englisch* world, and even if it were for the best of reasons, she had made a life there, even if it wasn't a happy one.

Sighing, he pushed himself away from the door with his arms and moved into the room. They'd had dinner, and Ellie was asleep. He prowled the room, unable to settle down.

He should try to get some sleep. Tomorrow would be a long day, no matter what. After all, how long could one expect a five-year-old to travel at the pace they were going without complaint.

He grinned. And Ellie could definitely complain. He was grateful his little one hadn't decided to throw a tantrum yet. The stubborn set of her chin and the way she pouted told him she had a streak of steel in her.

The grin faded away. She got that from her mother. His mind shifted to Christy. She was so strong, but he'd seen vulnerability, too. Especially when she'd talked of her family. She was very nonchalant about it, yet he'd seen the hurt that continued to lurk in her dark eyes.

Shaking his head, he sat on the bed and removed his boots. He wished his *daed* were there to give him advice. Or even one of his older brothers. Levi had left the Amish world for a while, but now he was back, and his faith had gotten him through so much. Then there was Abram, who'd been devastated when his childhood sweetheart had left him without a word.

Both men had struggled and both had stayed true to *Gott*, living the *Ordnung* as best they could. Now, both were happily married men starting their own families.

He closed his eyes but couldn't stop his mind from wondering if he'd ever be in that position.

He was stuck until he figured out what to do about Christy.

And maybe even after that.

Squeezing his eyes closed, he willed himself to relax, muscle by muscle, praying that he would find rest and some peace from his agonized thoughts.

Sam bolted upright, his brain foggy. For a few seconds, he couldn't remember where he was. Then he looked at the window. He'd left the curtain open and the neon sign outside was flashing Vacancy. He was at a hotel, and Christy and Ellie were safe in the room next door. He brushed his hands over his face to scrub away the sleep-induced haze. What had awakened him? He glanced at the clock. Just after four in the morning. He'd fallen into a restless doze somewhere in the neighborhood of midnight.

Slowly, he slipped his legs over the side of the bed, trying to be silent. He wasn't sure why, but he was moving on instinct now. He slipped his feet into his boots, not even bothering to tie the laces. Standing, he jammed his hat on his head. His senses were on high alert. Something was wrong.

Light from the parking lot lamps combined with the flashing sign filtered in through his window, creating myriad moving shadows. Was someone in the room with him? He held his breath. No other breathing or sounds surrounded him. Squinting, he scanned the darkness. Nothing was out of place. At least, nothing that he was aware of.

Something had awakened him, though.

There was a scratching sound at the door. Then the sound of the knob rattling. It could have been someone at the wrong door, but he knew it wasn't. Someone was attempting to open the door, probably trying to force the lock. It wouldn't have been Christy. If she needed him, she knew the connecting door was available. Adrenaline pumped through his blood. Following the outline of the bed, he moved around to the door that led to Christy's room. He opened it and slipped inside her room, shutting the door behind him and locking it.

Her room was much lighter than his due to the bathroom light being on.

As he neared the bed, she sat up. She must have already been awake, as she didn't startle or scream out at him. Her face was in shadows, but he imagined he could see the gleam of her brown eyes peering up at him.

"Sam?" Her whisper was harsh. He could feel the tension and fear emanating from her. Her voice was steady, though. She was so much stronger than he'd ever realized.

"We need to go. Now!" He pointed a thumb back at his room. "They've found us."

She understood immediately. Waking Ellie, she shushed the little girl's complaints before they started. "We have to go. No noise."

It broke his heart to see her sweet eyes pool with tears. Still, she didn't cry out. His daughter was brave, like her mother. He quickly kissed the top of her head to reassure her, then he gathered the boots beside the bed and bent to slide them onto her feet.

Something broke in his room. Someone swore, angrily. His glance met Christy's over Ellie's head.

They were out of time.

He grabbed a backpack and headed to the door. Placing his ear against it, he heard muttering in the hall. They were trapped. The men chasing them were waiting right outside the door.

Christy pulled him back and gestured to the window. She held on to his forearm and bounced up on her toes, leaning in so her lips touched his ear.

"Fire escape."

He ignored the shivers caused by her breath on his ear. Nothing mattered except getting them to safety.

Now would not be a good time to confess that she hated heights. It wasn't a phobia. Not exactly. After all, she'd managed to jump off a roof. A roof that had been much closer to the ground.

Sucking in a deep breath, Christy followed Sam out onto the narrow staircase. The metal landing swayed beneath her feet. Her stomach quailed in response.

She could do this. Grabbing the rusty railings in both hands, she took a step, shaking as the flimsy fire stairs wobbled beneath her feet. Sam and Ellie were already at the bottom. Panting, she kept her feet moving through sheer will.

"Christy! Look out!"

Sam's shout made her stumble as she turned.

Bryce glared down at her from where he'd climbed out onto the fire escape.

Gasping, she hurried down the ladder. Her foot missed the last step and she fell, landing in Sam's arms. He gripped her for a mere second before setting her down and picking up Ellie.

They dashed for the front of the building, footsteps stomping behind them. As they rounded the corner of the hotel, a gunshot burst from behind. Christy opened her mouth to pull in gulps of air. Her lungs were on fire as her airways swelled, inflamed from running in the extreme cold.

She was having an asthma attack and couldn't slow

down. Sam grabbed her hand and pulled her along. He looked down at her face and paled.

She gasped. "Can't…stop."

If I die, he has to protect Ellie.

The thought whirled through her panic-dazed mind as he grabbed her around the waist. With Ellie clinging on one side, their bags on his back, he half dragged her to the parking lot—toward a man with a long gray beard, in a red-and-black-checkered flannel shirt and a baseball cap, driving out in a Jeep.

Sam ran right in front of him.

"Help! We need help!"

The Jeep screeched to a halt.

That was all Sam needed. She would have laughed if she could have breathed. Sam shoved them into the Jeep.

"Hey now, fellow—" The man tried protesting.

"Drive!"

When a gunshot rang out, he slammed his foot to the floor and the Jeep roared out of the lot. He was muttering and spluttering, but didn't slow down. When they came to a yellow light, he blared the horn and raced through.

"You folks need to go to the police?"

Christy let Sam take point on the conversation. She buckled Ellie in as best she could without a booster seat, then began rooting around in her bag for her inhaler. When she pulled it out, she shook it to blend the albuterol inside the small canister before holding it to her lips and depressing the top while struggling to inhale. The first attempt loosened her airways only a tiny bit. She needed two more puffs before she could fully breathe again. The directions said only two puffs, but she didn't feel she had a choice.

Once she was able to get the oxygen she needed, Christy relaxed and tuned into the conversation happening in the front seat.

"We need to find a way back to my *haus*…"

The man whipped around a corner as if he were a teenager doing doughnuts in a parking lot. Dust, dirt and snow mingled in a dusky cloud behind them. It would have been humorous if there weren't killers coming to get them.

He plowed his Jeep through the snow and up a lane leading to a natural gas well, stopping behind a mound of gravel buried beneath the snow. Turning the key, the man shut down the engine and they paused. From their hidden position, they had a view of the main road, partially obscured by tree branches and other foliage.

They waited.

Even Ellie didn't make a sound, wide-eyed and trembling. Christy slid her arm around her little girl, giving her what comfort she could.

Two minutes later, an SUV whizzed past. It looked like the same one they had seen the day before, the one with the man who'd killed her sister. In the SUV's passenger seat, Christy could make out a hulking figure. She couldn't be sure, but her gut screamed it was Bryce. The bearded man he'd been with at her house was probably driving.

Although, she had no idea how many people were really caught up in the search for her and her daughter. And now Sam. That bothered her, the fact that she had dragged him into the mess with her. He didn't deserve it.

"That was them." Sam gestured to the now-empty road.

"You sure you don't want to go to the police?" The

older man restarted the vehicle. "I don't hold with anyone who'd hurt a young'un."

"Please." Christy leaned forward. "We just need to
get to Sam's home."

He didn't look happy about it. She had the feeling
Sam had told him enough of her story, though, that he
didn't question them too much. That was good. She
wasn't completely sanguine with being in a stranger's
Jeep, letting him drive them wherever he wanted. How
did they know he wouldn't head for the police station?

Her shoulders tensed. She turned slightly so she
could bounce her eyes between the front window and
the back one. Every minute, she expected to hear sirens or to see an SUV tailing them.

Neither happened.

When he finally pulled into an old farmhouse yard,
she sank against the leather seat, exhausted from the
fifteen-minute ride. He rumbled past the silo, the Jeep
swaying and lurching on the uneven gravel driveway.
At the speed he was driving, she was shocked he didn't
break off the muffler in one of the dips in the drive.

Christy bit her lip. She needed to be thankful that
he'd brought them to a home rather than turn them in.

She knew many people wouldn't have taken the
word of a stranger. But she supposed a woman with
a child traveling with an Amish fellow didn't appear
dangerous.

The man backed the Jeep into a space beside the
barn and motioned for them to follow him. "I don't
mind feeding you breakfast while you plan."

Sam helped her and Ellie from the Jeep.

Approaching the house, Christy's throat constricted.
Inside, there was a Christmas tree positioned in the

center of the picture window at the front of the house. Regardless of the fact that it was early in the day, hundreds of lights twinkled and blazed in the branches.

A mock stable, built beside the porch, contained a nativity scene. She'd almost forgotten, despite the displays in the shops in town, that it was less than three weeks until Christmas. Would she be able to celebrate with Ellie? Her daughter was old enough to be excited about Christmas.

The farmer ushered them into the house. They kicked the snow from their boots before crossing the threshold. Inside, there was a small rug topped with pairs of shoes. Following unspoken protocol, they shed their boots and hung their coats on the pegs nailed to the wall.

From close up, she could see that the Christmas tree was decorated with what looked like handmade ornaments. Probably made by his children over the years. The smell of fresh-baked banana bread lingered in the air.

"Thank you for helping us," Christy said.

He pointed to Ellie. "I got a granddaughter 'bout her age. Don't get to see her as much as I'd like. My daughter's husband is a military man and they're stationed in Texas right now. I know if someone were shooting at my Daria, I'd want someone to give 'em a hand. Least we Christians can do."

She nodded over the lump in her throat.

"Appreciate it." Sam's voice sounded scratchy. Was he, too, overwhelmed by this man's kindness?

A woman entered the room, drying her hands on a towel.

"This here's my bride, Opal." The woman blushed and grinned at him.

Christy smiled, warmed by the affection between them. They had to be in their fifties or so, but the look they shared was pure love. It was charming. And it tugged at her soul. Once, she would have said she and Sam would have looked at each other like that when they were older.

"Grant Stewart," his wife chided. "How you carry on!" She then smiled at her guests. "Ignore my husband. We've been married thirty-one years."

Grant introduced them and told her a bit of their story.

"You poor things!" Opal bustled everyone into the kitchen. "Let's get some breakfast in your bellies, then you all can sit and plan."

Soon, they were sitting down to farm-fresh eggs, toast, bacon, and the best coffee Christy had ever sipped. She held a large mug in both hands and inhaled, closing her eyes to savor the rich aroma.

"Mommy!" Ellie's squeal had both Sam and Christy jumping out of their chairs.

Ellie didn't notice. Her delighted gaze was glued to a spot under the table. A large gray cat with a round face was rubbing against her legs, purring loudly.

Grant chuckled. "That's Oliver. He and his sister, Jazzy, rule this house. Or at least they think they do."

Christy and Sam sank back into their chairs. She placed a hand over her heart, trying to slow its frantic beat. Sam, she noticed, was pale. They exchanged weak smiles, both relieved that the danger they'd expected hadn't been found.

Opal looked at Ellie. "You know, I think we might

have some clothes that our older granddaughters have outgrown. We could find her something clean."

Christy couldn't agree fast enough and within minutes, Ellie was wearing a fresh pair of jeans, thick socks and a lovely pink blouse under a fuzzy turtleneck sweater.

Opal threw all their coats, hats and clothes into the wash.

After Opal was satisfied that she'd done what she needed to, she took Ellie upstairs to meet the other cat. Ellie's delighted squeal floated down the stairs and echoed against the wooden floors. Grant, Christy and Sam all laughed.

"If I were to guess, I'd say Opal will also show her the toys that we keep here for the grandkids. We should have an hour or so to talk."

Christy turned on her phone to pull up the maps. Her battery was at twenty-seven percent, so she connected the charger and plugged it in while they devised the best way for them to travel.

Her phone was charged and their coats hanging on the hooks again when the door opened and a young man around their age entered the house through the connected garage.

He took one look at Christy and his jaw dropped.

"Hey! I've seen you! Your brother was in town, searching for you."

EIGHT

The blood rushed from her head and Christy swayed on her feet. Aghast, she stared at the young man standing before her as he calmly chomped on his chewing gum. "My brother? I don't have a brother."

If he only knew the truth about who was searching for her!

He scratched the back of his head and frowned. "Really? That's strange. He had a picture of you and everything. He said you'd taken off with your kid and some riffraff."

When Sam cleared his throat, the newcomer flushed, realizing his faux pas. "Sorry, dude. I'm just repeating what I heard them say in town. I don't mean to offend anyone."

Christy waved her hand, dismissing the apology. "It doesn't matter. Please describe the man you saw."

"He was taller than me. Bulky, like he worked out. Crew cut. A nose that looked like it'd been in a few fights in his life." He shifted his weight then shrugged. "I didn't talk to him. He was showing your picture to the man at the convenience store. The guy said he'd not seen you."

"William, what store were you at?" his father asked.

The youth gave the name of an unfamiliar chain.

"They're getting closer." Grant shoved his chair back and stood. "When they passed us, they were heading away from us. That store, however, means they're still in the area. I had hoped they'd have kept going."

William's mouth pursed. "You're getting in a little deep with these people, don't you think, Dad? For all we know, they could be thieves or con men." He shifted his glance to Christy. "Con people."

Christy sniffed. Really, what sorts of con artists bring a young child with them?

"We can't stay here," Sam moved closer to her side and touched her elbow. "Christy, we have to go."

She heard the apology in his voice and nodded, placing her hand over his briefly to let him know she understood. He'd hoped for a short respite for them, so they could refresh, regain their balance.

"It's okay," she whispered.

Sam flipped his hand over and caught hers in a gentle grip. He squeezed and released it so quickly, she might have missed it if she hadn't been paying attention. She missed the sensation of his skin. It comforted her more than she could ever have imagined.

Glimpsing Grant's scowl at his son, she knew what they had to do.

"Grant, we appreciate your help, but we have to leave. We can't put you in any more danger. We thank you for your kindness."

He opened his mouth, like he was going to protest, then snapped it shut. "I suppose you're right. You guys need to go. Don't want to risk any killers getting to you."

William's cocky expression melted and his complexion had turned ashen. "Killers! Dad, are you serious?" His panicked gaze swiveled from one face to another.

Christy sympathized, but she didn't have time to explain. She had to get her daughter ready.

Running to the stairs, she called for Ellie. Within seconds, the child skipped to the stairs, a silky black cat under one arm and doll in the other.

"Ellie. Hurry, honey. We have to go."

The happy smile dissolved and temper snapped in her eyes. Her lips pushed out in a pout. "Don't want to go. I like it here. Mommy, I want a cat."

"Eleanor Samantha."

Ellie lowered her gaze. Christy didn't often get stern with her daughter, but she wouldn't tolerate disobedience, especially not at a time like this.

Despondent, the child tromped down the steps, the cat meowing in protest. At the bottom of the stairs, the feline scrambled and made a bid for freedom. Ellie dropped her, crying.

Christy's heart twisted inside her chest. It wasn't a cat getting away that caused Ellie's tears. It was this whole mess their lives had become these past three days. Since Tuesday evening, Ellie had missed two days of school, of seeing her friends and teachers. She'd missed being able to play freely and to be happy. Or as happy as Christy had been able to make her childhood.

She'd never get those days back. Who knew how many more days they'd be on the run?

Or if they'd even survive.

Stop it! She refused to allow her mind to go there.

Hope. She had to continue to hope and believe. Tears flooded her eyes as she looked at her child.

A strong arm eased around her shoulders and pulled her close until she was nestled against Sam's side. "It will be well, Christy. *Gott* has a plan. He will care for us and guide us."

She so wanted to believe that.

"How do you know?" She kept her voice low, not wanting Grant or William to overhear. "He didn't help us six years ago."

His lips touched her ear. "How do you know that He wasn't guiding us even then? We can't always know. We have to have faith."

Faith. Did she even know what that really meant? Why was she letting him get this close? Every time he breathed on her ear, or touched her, her pulse fluttered and her stomach got all wobbly inside. She was setting herself up for a broken heart. It was time she smartened up.

She shrugged his arm off her shoulders. "I don't have time for this."

Opal appeared at the top of the stairs and ambled toward them. Her mouth turned down at the corners as she neared them. "I heard you talking. You're leaving, then?"

They nodded.

She fingered Ellie's hair. "I wish you well."

Sam and Christy were silent as they bundled up and helped a resistant Ellie into her snow clothes again. At least they'd been fed and had some clean clothes for their daughter. Opal had found a small bear, only a couple of inches tall, and had given it to Ellie.

Christy's eyes misted at the gesture.

They were ready to leave.

Opal looked out the window. "Grant, do we know anyone who drives a black SUV?"

Sam and Christy froze, their eyes meeting over Ellie's head in horror.

"It's Bryce."

Sam couldn't stand the hopelessness in Christy's voice.

"Daddy!"

He bent and lifted his daughter into his arms. "I'm here, Ellie. Your *mamm* and I are both here, and we'll keep you safe."

He so wanted to believe that. He needed to do what he'd lectured Christy about. Times like these called for decisive action and unwavering faith. He silently prayed for both.

"Opal, we'll get the door. William, I need you to lead Sam, Christy and their daughter out to the shed behind the barn. The three of them can hide there," Grant said.

William didn't like it. Sam could see that. To his credit, the young man did as he was told.

Quickly, he donned his own boots. "This way."

Still holding Ellie, Sam followed William through the kitchen to the door leading to the garage. He could feel Christy behind him but couldn't prevent himself from turning to check on her every few steps. A thin trail of sweat formed on his brow and trickled down his face. He ignored it.

Opening the door, William led them into the garage. They crouch-walked along the wall, even as they could hear someone banging on the farmhouse door.

Grant and Opal didn't answer the door. Sam wondered what had happened. Not that he minded. He didn't think letting those thugs in the *haus* was the wise thing to do in any circumstance.

Exiting through the door at the rear of the garage that led to the backyard, they realized they could hear the men talking.

"I know they have to be here," one man muttered. "Look at all these cars. This is where we tracked them to."

"Yeah, but don't be too sure. We lost her phone signal again. I think either the battery died or she shut it off."

A snicker. "It was brilliant of O'Malley to put a tracking device in her phone."

A tracking device! That was how they kept finding them.

Sam remembered that Christy had turned on her phone that morning to charge it and to check the maps. He sent a glance her way. Her face was bloodless, but her eyes blazed with fury. Without a word, Christy dropped her shoulder to let her backpack fall forward. Still wordless, she opened it and pulled out the offending device. Revulsion twisted her lovely features. He had never seen her lose her composure this much.

"I need to get rid of this thing." Her breath misted in front of her face.

"There's a burn barrel out back." William lifted his right arm and gestured to a cloud of smoke rising beyond the barn. "I started it this morning. There should be enough flame left to do some damage."

It took a few minutes to reach the barn, sneaking the way they were. When they finally reached the back,

Christy marched to the burn barrel. Sparks and embers were still shooting from within it, although much of the blaze had died down. She held the phone between her fingers as if it were poisonous and dropped it in the flames.

When she turned around, her expression was one of resolve. This was another betrayal. Sam had no doubt that the O'Malley they'd talked about was her father. He'd put a tracker in her phone. Why? Had he planned to kill her or was there another reason?

Whatever it was, Sam couldn't fathom it.

Suddenly, he missed the simplicity of his Plain life more than he'd believed possible. If only he could return and have his daughter and Christy with him, he'd be content. As it was, he needed to guard his heart from longing for what could never be.

William and Sam didn't say a word as they all moved to the handmade shed behind the barn.

William opened the door and let them slip inside.

"We can hole up in here for a short time," he murmured. "When they've gone, you can take one of our vehicles. We have plenty. We'll worry about getting it back at a later date. Not a huge concern right now."

Ellie began to sniffle. Sam nuzzled her cheek and muttered softly to her.

"I don't think she understands Pennsylvania Dutch," Christy said as she leaned her head against his arm.

The simple gesture of trust took his breath away. It also distracted his thoughts for a moment. "I didn't realize I was talking in Pennsylvania Dutch. I was attempting to soothe her."

"I think it worked."

He looked down. Ellie had stuck her thumb in her

mouth and curled up against his chest, eyes closed. She may not have understood the German-based dialect he spoke at home with his family, but she had apparently understood the sentiments he'd intended to relay.

"She hasn't sucked her thumb in a long time."

Sam grimaced. "No doubt all the stress of the past few days, *jah*?"

"Yeah. Once we put this unpleasantness behind us, she should stop again."

A banging noise from somewhere outside silenced all conversation. A second noise, muffled, was closer this time.

"Someone's in the barn." William's whisper was little more than a breath.

They waited. Christy trembled beside him. Was this it? Maybe hiding in the shed hadn't been the best idea. There was no back door. The only way out was the door they'd entered through.

They stood in the dark for several long minutes. Sam held Ellie close. When she moved restlessly, he tightened his hold. Christy moved, hooking one arm behind his back to anchor herself, the other one embracing their daughter from the front. They stood together, just breathing.

Gott, deliver us. Save us.

After what felt like an hour, William moved. "I think they're done. It's been twenty-one minutes."

Sam relaxed his hold. When Christy slid her arms away, he wanted to reclaim them, which would have been foolish. She had her life to live, and it was totally removed from his.

He hoped they could be free from this danger soon. Even if it destroyed his chances of happiness for himself, he'd gladly accept that prognosis if it meant his daughter and Christy were safe.

"You guys stay here." William started to open the door. "I'm going to go check on my parents. I don't like leaving them alone in the house. Who knows what those dudes will do when they don't find you?"

Christy shifted. She was feeling the weight of the responsibility if anything happened to their hosts. Sam knew because he felt it, too. "I'll go with you—" he started to say.

He stopped when a quiet explosion burst from inside the *haus*, followed a second later by a second blast. Then the air was filled with the unmistakable sounds of men shouting and feet pounding across a wooden porch. William staggered briefly then attacked the shed door, bursting through it at a run even as the SUV zoomed down the drive and roared away.

Sam thrust Ellie into Christy's arms. "Stay here!"

He didn't wait for her to respond, but took off after William. Grant and Opal had been in the *haus* alone with Bryce. He knew exactly what the blasts had been.

Gunshots.

Two of them.

One for each of their hosts.

NINE

Sam and William raced for the *haus*, slipping and sliding in their rush to reach Grant and Opal. They were still twenty feet from the door when they heard Opal cry out for help. Tucking his chin down, he leaned into his stride to force himself to run faster. Blood was spattered across the porch and down the steps, leaving a morbid red path to where the SUV had been parked. That gave him pause.

One of the villains had been injured. Unless they'd kidnapped Grant. He could hear Opal's voice inside the *haus*.

They reached the *haus* and William nearly tore the screen door off its hinges in his desperation to reach his parents.

Sam stumbled in behind him, panting. His knee throbbed slightly. He must have twisted it in his haste.

Grant was lying on the floor in the hall, three feet from the front door. A pool of blood was spreading across the hardwood beneath him. He was moaning, his hand clutching his side. A twelve-gauge shotgun lay on the floor, inches from his feet.

Opal ran in from the kitchen, towels in her arms.

She dropped to her side beside her husband, yanked his shirt up and pressed a clean towel against his wound. She was competent, and the gaze she leveled on William and Sam was pure steel.

"I've called 9-1-1. Those goons came in to find you and Christy, Sam. Grant had hidden the shotgun nearby, but we couldn't make any sudden moves to grab it. They started off with the spiel about looking for their lost sister, just like William had said. When they realized we wouldn't help them, they got mad. That's when the big guy pulled out a gun. The other two guys went to search for you. They were gone for about ten minutes or so before they returned to say he hadn't found anything."

"Mom, we heard two shots."

"Yeah, you did." She continued tending Grant and didn't look up. A thread of satisfaction oozed into her voice. "When they came back, the big one was spitting mad. He shot Grant out of pure spite. Then one of the other guys started hollering at him. He said 'no witnesses.' I ran to the gun and shot the one who'd hit your dad in the leg. Told them I'd take them both out."

"They've left." Sam knelt on one knee next to Grant. "I am so sorry."

Grant grimaced. It looked like an attempt at a smile. "This isn't your fault."

Startled, Sam looked at William. Somehow, he thought the son would have been the first to blame them for bringing such misery on their family.

"He's right." Opal tilted her head. He could hear sirens.

"You go back to the shed." William jerked his head toward the door. "I'll come and get you after the ambulance and police leave. Then you can take my truck, as we planned."

Sam wanted to say more, to express his sorrow and appreciation, but there was no time. He needed to be out of the *haus* when the emergency personal arrived.

He barely made it, slipping out of sight as the first vehicle pulled in. He hid inside the barn and watched while the ambulance crew pulled out a stretcher and carried it up the porch. From where he was hiding, he could see them pause and visually track the blood trail. They were still standing there when the *Englisch* police arrived. Two officers exited their vehicles and strode to where the ambulance crew stood. He couldn't hear their conversation, but knew they were talking about the blood spattered over the snow and the porch.

He couldn't move while they were standing there. Any noise or movement could lead them to him, which would lead them to Christy and Ellie. He wasn't sure what to think. It was likely they'd help her, especially with the actions the killers had committed today. But he couldn't risk it.

It took them forever to leave the porch. The ambulance crew went inside, along with one of the officers. The other stood outside for a few minutes, using his phone to take pictures of the blood trail, and talking to someone on the radio hooked to his shoulder.

Sam's leg started to cramp. He ground his teeth, trying to ignore the pain.

Finally, the officer headed into the *haus* to join the others.

He needed to move, now. He had no idea how long he had until they headed outside. Making his way to the back, he exited through the main door near the rear of the barn.

Entering the shed, he saw Christy blink up into the sudden light. The fear on her face gripped his heart like a giant fist. She clutched Ellie, making the child whine in protest.

She couldn't see him, he realized. The sudden change in light hadn't given her eyes time to adjust.

"It's *gut*, Christy. It's me, Sam."

She let a out breath, like air whooshing from a popped balloon, and her posture wilted.

"You terrified me."

He shut the door, once more locking them into the darkness.

"Grant? Opal?" Her voice quavered in the space between them. "Are they all right?"

"Opal is fine. Grant was shot."

She gasped, the sound harsh in the quiet space. "Oh no! How bad?"

He heard the horror in her voice. He scooted over so he could take Christy and Ellie in his arms as they talked. "I don't know how bad. William is with them."

"I heard sirens."

"*Jah.* The *Englisch* police and an ambulance are here. We're supposed to wait until they leave. We'll know more soon."

But first they had to wait. He sat on the floor, gently tugging them down with him. Ellie, probably exhausted from their ordeal, drifted into sleep. He kissed her head, silently promising her to do what he could to protect her.

The vision of blood pooling under Grant's body and Opal trying to stem the flow was imprinted on his mind. He'd never forget that image. His mind was steeped in his guilt and the horror of the events.

He shook his head. *Nee.* He had to keep his mind clear. They were still in trouble. Grant and Opal had known they were being chased; they hadn't hid the truth from them.

But still, he couldn't dislodge the sense that he and Christy were to blame.

"We're not to blame."

Startled, he peered through the darkness to where Christy's voice had come from. Had he said the words out loud?

"*Jah*, I know. But I feel guilty." He was so tired. Sam leaned his head back against the wooden side of the shed.

"I know." Her hand tentatively touched his. He flopped his hand over and gripped hers. "I feel guilty, too. But I didn't ask for this. Neither did you. Or Jo Anne. I have to remember that I am not at fault for the things my father has done."

Christy allowed her hand to remain in his. The warmth and comfort of his touch was a balm to her wounded and weary soul. The feeling of not being alone washed over her. It brought its own sort of peace, although she was still worried about what was to come.

Sitting on the ground, she shivered.

"So, what happens now?" She leaned her head against Sam's shoulder, soaking in his warmth.

"We wait. William will come and get us when it's safe."

"Hmm. I'm a bit surprised he's being helpful." William hadn't struck her as happy with all that was happening at his house. "Do you think he'll betray our presence to the police?"

If he thought they were at fault, he might feel justified.

"*Nee*, I don't. He doesn't like this, but I trust him."

Why, she wanted to ask. How could he trust so easily? She didn't know if she had it in her to open up any further.

"I can't believe my dad put a tracking device in my phone." She hadn't meant to say that. Now that she had, though, the heat of her anger was burning a hole in her gut. Dads were supposed to protect their children, like Sam was doing with Ellie.

What kind of father puts a tracking device in their daughter's phone so that killers could hunt her down?

The evil of it choked her. Her shudder had nothing to do with the cold invading her limbs.

"*Jah*. I was shocked, too. It makes sense, though. I'd been wondering how the killers kept finding us, no matter where we went."

She nodded her head against his shoulder. "Yeah. Me, too. I thought I'd been smart, turning off the location settings. It never occurred to me that there'd been a tracking device."

"One *gut* thing. Now that you've destroyed the phone, they won't be able to use the tracker anymore, ain't so?"

Sam was optimistic, that was certain. For herself, she was quickly losing her positive attitude.

"Yeah, but it also means no map. And no way to call 9-1-1 if we need to."

He shrugged, the motion jarring her head slightly. She chuckled. "Hey. You're moving my cushion."

He huffed a laugh. "Sorry. I'll try to be more careful."

The laugh died out.

They sighed in unity and let the silence settle around them like a blanket.

The sound of steps tromping through the snow alerted them to someone's presence. She stiffened. Sam straightened and handed Ellie to her. Ellie didn't stir and Christy enveloped her in her arms. She'd protect this child or die trying.

The door jerked open, flooding the shed with bright light. She blinked and turned her head from the light. It took a few seconds for her eyes to begin to adjust. Squinting, she tilted her head to get a better look in her periphery.

William stood in the doorway.

Sam took Ellie back before helping Christy to her feet. She cried out as the sensation of hundreds of needles prickled her numb legs. Staggering, she crashed into Sam. He didn't budge.

"You okay?"

"Yep. My leg went to sleep." She peered at William. "How…?" She stopped, unsure if she could ask.

He smiled at her, a weak smile, but there was no malice or accusation in it. "My dad's going to be fine. He'll be in the hospital for a couple of days, but then he'll be home. My mom's a rock. She'll stay with him as much as she can."

He waved for them to come out of the shed.

"I'm going to lend you my truck. I gassed it up this morning, so you should be good to go. It'll take you about two and a half hours to get to Sutter Springs.

Maybe a little less. You should be there early afternoon."

"William, are you sure?" Sam took the keys he held out and passed them to Christy. She'd be the one doing the driving. "We've caused you enough trouble."

She rolled her eyes. Hadn't they already talked about this?

Shaking his head, William began walking toward the house, motioning for them to follow. "Nah. This is absolutely not your fault. I'm not happy that it happened, but my parents aren't fools. They have good heads on their shoulders. If they felt that you were in trouble and needed help, then that's all there was to it. I'm sorry it happened, but it could have been so much worse."

He was taking this much better than she would have. *It is what Christians do.*

Ellie stirred awake, demanding to be put down. Sam set her on her feet. She stomped in the snow as they walked. Not mad, just liking the way the snow puffed around her boots as she moved. Christy had seen her do this many times.

Once inside the house, the little girl immediately found Oliver and Jazzy and became entranced with playing with the cats. Christy didn't mind. It gave the child something innocent to focus on for a few minutes.

She followed behind the men, only half listening to William giving instructions on his truck. She was in the middle of a spiritual crisis.

She'd never had an example to learn from. Had never understood what it meant to be a Christian. Even when she'd met Sam, he'd spoken of faith, and she'd had a spark of interest. But before she could learn, truly learn, about his faith, her father had appeared and swept her back to the life she'd been so desperate to escape.

She sighed. Sam had been the first Amish person she'd ever known. Sure, she'd seen the Amish before. And she'd seen their buggies on the roads when she'd traveled. But she'd never talked with anyone who was Amish before. Had never even really been curious. Her whole life had been filled with drama and tension. All she had wanted was escape.

Had she used Sam to try to escape?

Her stomach twisted. She was growing to appreciate him now in a way she never had before. His calmness, his dedication to her and to Christy, even while he knew they had no future. She liked the little bit of adventure she'd seen in his gaze, the way he made her feel special when he touched her hand.

Six years ago, she'd been fleeing her father's house and hadn't really taken the time to know Sam and what was important to him. The shallowness of that time made her cringe inside.

Was the way Sam put her and Ellie before his own wishes…was that the way of a Christian? He was resolved to abide by the rules of his church at a time when many people disregarded rules because they considered them inconvenient.

She liked that he was resolute. She liked it a lot. Her world was full of people who said one thing and did another. It impressed her that he did exactly what he promised. And that he never seemed to place blame on anyone else. Even now, he was unafraid to accept responsibility for what had happened with Grant and Opal.

He was a man she could respect.

She hadn't met many men she respected. Or women, for that matter.

What a waste!

"I need to get to the hospital." William shrugged into a clean coat. The one he'd worn earlier was on the floor with bloodstains on it. "Help yourselves to whatever is in the fridge. And if you think of it, give me a call when everything is done to let us know you're safe. My folks would like to know that their help paid off."

He scribbled a number on a sticky note and handed it to Christy. She shoved it into her back pocket and said, "Will do. When we can, and are able to find a phone, that is."

A ghost of a grin crossed William's face. She looked at Sam. He had a similar expression.

"What?" She'd obviously missed the joke.

"Nothing." Sam's face broke into a wide smile. She caught her breath as a dimple flashed. "I'm just remembering your face as you tossed your phone onto the fire."

"I don't see why that's funny."

Really, it was a horrible situation.

His face softened. "Christy, I'm not smiling because it was funny. You were amazing."

"I agree," William added. "I don't know anyone who would so casually throw away an expensive phone. You didn't even blink an eye."

Yeah, she'd known people who would have balked at tossing a phone away, too.

"Well, it's only a thing. Protecting my family and your parents was more important."

"Can't argue."

William saluted them and departed through the garage door. A few seconds later, she heard a hum as the door lifted. He started his car and left.

Christy was standing in the kitchen with Sam. He had a peculiar expression on his face, but she didn't have time to figure it out. She rushed around the kitchen, searching for nonperishable food items to take with them. She had no idea how long they'd be on the road, even though it should only be a couple of hours. The last two days had showed her how easily plans could and would go awry.

Soon, she had gathered up bottled water, peanut butter and jelly sandwiches, some fruit, graham crackers and mixed nuts. She found some disposable coffee cups with lids. She hesitated for only a second before using two of the Stewarts' K-cups to make coffee for her and Sam. She didn't know about him, but she needed the caffeine to remain alert.

Ten minutes later, she was ready to travel. As they ushered an unhappy Ellie to the truck, Christy thought back to what she'd told Sam and William. Ellie and Sam were her family. The only true family she had left, in her opinion. Regardless of her marital status, Sam was important to her, and to Ellie.

She got into the truck and adjusted the seat and the mirrors. As she did so, she remembered Sam's quiet prayer earlier. Inspired, she decided to try it herself.

God, if You're really there. Please protect us.

She felt foolish, but at the same time, relieved. If they were going to make it out of this alive, they would need God on their side. If he would listen to Christy, after she'd ignored Him her whole life.

TEN

Sam tapped his fingers on the plastic windowsill and watched the scenery flash by. He couldn't get Christy's words out of his mind.

Family. She considered him family. Did he feel the same way? Granted, they were connected by a rather extraordinary past. Not to mention the most adorable daughter a man could ever want.

But family?

Jah, she was family. They might be married, maybe not. But that didn't matter. Their bond was real.

Not that it changed anything. He still couldn't envision a future that would allow them to be together. It worried him. As much as he wanted to keep his distance, every hour in her presence seemed only to tighten those bonds.

How would he ever be free of her?

"Why did you agree to marry me six years ago?"

Startled out of his reverie, he shifted his position so he could see her better. The sunlight coming in through the window made her hair glow with fiery golden highlights he'd never noticed before. Her face was still smooth, even after all she'd been through. It

Loyal Readers
FREE BOOKS Voucher

We're giving away **THOUSANDS** of **FREE BOOKS**

Romance

Suspense

Get up to 4
FREE FABULOUS BOOKS
You Love!

To thank you for being a loyal reader we'd like to send you up to 4 FREE BOOKS, absolutely free.

Just write "YES" on the Loyal Reader Voucher and we'll send you up to 4 Free Books and Free Mystery Gifts, altogether worth over $20, as a way of saying thank you for being a loyal reader.

Try **Love Inspired® Romance Larger-Print** books and fall in love with inspirational romances that take you on an uplifting journey of faith, forgiveness and hope.

Try **Love Inspired® Suspense Larger-Print** books where courage and optimism unite in stories of faith and love in the face of danger.

Or **TRY BOTH!**

We are so glad you love the books as much as we do and can't wait to send you great new books.

So don't miss out, return your Loyal Reader Voucher Today!

Pam Powers

LOYAL READER
FREE BOOKS VOUCHER

YES! I Love Reading, please send me up to 4 FREE BOOKS and Free Mystery Gifts from the series I select.

Just write in "YES" on the dotted line below then return this card today and we'll send your free books & gifts asap!

➡ YES ⬅
_ _ _ _

Which do you prefer?

| | Love Inspired® Romance Larger-Print 122/322 IDL GRJD | | Love Inspired® Suspense Larger-Print 107/307 IDL GRJD | | **BOTH** 122/322 & 107/307 IDL GRJP |

FIRST NAME

LAST NAME

ADDRESS

APT.#

CITY

STATE/PROV.

ZIP/POSTAL CODE

EMAIL ☐ Please check this box if you would like to receive newsletters and promotional emails from Harlequin Enterprises ULC and its affiliates. You can unsubscribe anytime.

LI/SLI-520-LR21

was in her dark eyes, however, where one could see the pain and secrets she held lurking. She squinted into the glare of the sun reflecting off the snow.

"You know why. We were young and in love."

She shrugged. "Maybe. But I wonder how much of it was because you were rebelling."

"*Nee.* I was acting out, *jah*, but I would never have taken such a drastic step just to defy my *daed.* I wanted us to be together."

She pursed her lips. He needed to explain things better.

"When I was a kid, I was very shy. And I hated confrontation. Of any kind."

She glanced his way briefly. "I can't see it."

"It's true. I told you my brother Levi left after an argument with my father, *jah*?"

"I remember." Her quiet response was accompanied by a swift, concerned glance. "You don't have to say anything if you don't want to. I didn't mean to pry."

He appreciated the regret in her voice. It was a touchy subject, one he didn't speak of easily. In this instance, the need to unburden himself rose inside him, ready to boil over. Who else would understand?

Besides, he knew about her family. It was nothing less than fair that he should confess about his.

"I don't mind." He leaned his head back and pounded a fist lightly on his thigh. "My best friend had stolen some money from his *daed*'s shop. I don't know how it started, but Martin would take a few dollars a week."

"He was embezzling from his father?"

He winced at the word. "*Jah.* My brother was working at the shop part-time. He'd expressed some interest in becoming a carpenter rather than joining the painting business. My *daed* wasn't pleased. He wanted all of us to join the business."

She didn't say anything but nodded.

"It didn't take long for Martin's *daed* to notice the missing money. Or to accuse Levi. Except, he didn't accuse him. He told my *daed* that Levi was stealing, without actually talking to my brother. Levi has always had a keen sense of what was right. He would never have taken the money. What neither of them knew was that when I was at the shop the week before, I saw Martin take some money. I confronted him, which was not my way. He was my best friend, so I felt duty-bound to point out the error of his ways."

"What did he say?"

"He promised to confess. When I heard Levi's argument with *Daed*, I realized Martin had never done it. I confronted him again, told him about the argument. He promised to tell his *daed* the truth, but never did. He let his *daed* believe it was Levi."

She sucked in a shocked breath.

"I went to my *daed* and told him what I'd seen. He immediately approached Martin's *daed*, who tried to accuse me of lying. Me!" He snorted. "I couldn't believe it. Martin finally confessed, but only after *Daed* got the bishop involved. By then, it was too late. Levi had left. It was a long time before I could forgive my *daed* or Martin. We still aren't more than nodding acquaintances."

"You say it took a long time to forgive your father," she said slowly, her voice careful, as if she worried she might be overstepping.

"*Jah*. But I did, and *Daed* and I have a solid relationship."

"I'm glad of that. What I want to know is, have you forgiven yourself?"

His jaw dropped as he blinked at her. Forgiven himself? "What?"

The smile she aimed at him was affectionate with a measure of exasperation thrown in. "It's obvious to me. You still blame yourself on some level for your brother's suffering. Which is ridiculous, although I understand it."

His mind reeled. Could it be true? Had he blamed himself? His brother's flight had certainly affected him.

"I guess I have blamed myself. If I had gone to my father and told him what I knew then Levi wouldn't have left."

"Yeah, but how do you know this wasn't part of God's plan?"

He laughed in disbelief. "Are you talking about *Gott*'s plan? I thought you weren't a believer."

She brushed an impatient hand through her hair. "I don't know what I believe. But I know you tell me that I have to trust. I kind of think you should follow your own advice."

For an instant, he stiffened, insulted. After a moment of thought, he let his offended feelings go. "You're right. I should." He grinned at her suddenly. "I'll make a believer of you yet."

She shook with a silent chuckle. "You can try. I'm not convinced yet. But you can try."

It was almost one in the afternoon when they pulled into Sutter Springs. He straightened in his seat as he saw the familiar buildings and landscapes, and pointed out different landmarks. They drove around the lake and past the Plain and Simple Bed and Breakfast owned by his *onkel* and *aenti*.

"You talked with my cousin Adele when you called. She was shocked, to say the least."

Christy grimaced. "Sorry about that. I had to convince you to come. I didn't think of any trouble I could get you into."

"That's more my fault than yours. You had no way of knowing I had left them in the dark."

His mood grew tense as they approached his family's *haus*. The muscles in his stomach tightened. He had never meant to mislead his family, but he had. Now he'd have to own up to his past mistakes and face the consequences.

He groaned as they pulled into the driveway. Abram's buggy was in the yard. He loved his brother, but he didn't relish spilling his darkest secret in front of any of his siblings before he'd informed his parents.

Or the bishop. Internally, he squirmed at the idea. He would need for extra courage for that one.

Gott, please guide me and give me strength.

He wanted to pray for a positive outcome, but didn't think it was appropriate to ask *Gott* to help him avoid the direct consequences of his actions. A little voice whispered that it was hard to be completely sorry since Ellie had come of his actions.

He had been wrong, but his daughter was everything that was precious and *gut*.

"There are no decorations." Christy followed his directions and passed the *haus*, driving toward the barn.

"We don't put up decorations like the *Englisch*

do. No lights or Santa or reindeer. We're simple folk. Maybe a few candles. Some greens."

She scanned the area, her eyes resting on the candles in the windows. A small smile played around her mouth. "I like it. Vanessa always went all-out with the decorations, but the holiday itself was empty at our house."

The truck ground to a halt in front of the barn. Without speaking, the small family exited. Sam gathered the backpacks and Christy helped Ellie out.

"Mommy," Ellie whispered, "there's a horsey!" The child pointed at the mare, calmly walking in the field, and scrunched her cute little nose. "Why's the horsey wearing a coat?"

Sam chuckled. "It's a horse blanket to keep her warm. It's cold out, even for the animals."

Her hazel eyes widened at this news.

"We've never been allowed a pet." Christy smoothed her daughter's hair and readjusted her hat. "Vanessa disliked animals."

He didn't know what he could say to that. Most Amish didn't have indoor pets, but he'd always had animals around the barn. They were a part of his life.

"*Cumme.* Let's go inside." He moved to the back door of the house and held it open for them. After they'd divested themselves of their hats, boots and coats, he led them into the front room where his family was gathered.

Mamm, *Daed*, Abram and Katie, Abram's wife, all turned to smile as he entered the room. His parents' smiles faltered as Christy and Ellie followed him. Abram's face became shuttered, speculation in his eyes. Katie's gaze narrowed, but her smile never dimmed.

"Sam." David Burkholder approached him, his eyes

still on their guests. "Adele told us you had gone to assist a friend in Shipshewana?" His father's tone was
thick with questions.

A small gasp caught Sam's attention. He looked
down to see Ellie staring up at David Burkholder,
her mouth and eyes wide in terror as his gentle *daed*
walked closer. Her gaze had zeroed in on his father's
face. More particularly, on the long beard that all
Amish men begin to grow when they marry.

Instinctively, Sam edged closer to the small child
to comfort her. She lurched forward and grabbed his
hand in both of hers, huddling half behind him, her
eyes peering out at his *daed*.

"Daddy, I'm scared!"

His *mamm* gasped.

A heavy silence permeated the room. All eyes
zoomed in on Christy and Ellie.

Christy squirmed as Sam's family continued to stare
at her. She could read the shock in his parents' eyes.

Maybe this hadn't been a good idea, after all.

She maintained her silence, though. This was not
her family. If she were to be offered sanctuary here,
it was up to Sam to make it happen. Squirming a bit
inside, she took a page out of Sam's book and offered
up a quick prayer for things to go smooth. Then she
flushed. She was an impostor, standing in this Amish
home praying like she was a believer.

Although, she could no longer claim she wasn't. It
wasn't a comfortable feeling.

"*Sohn*, I think you might have some explaining to
do." His father's voice rumbled out, surprising her
with the lack of heat in it. She expected to hear anger,

maybe even some yelling. Instead, his voice was gentle and low. They could have been talking about anything.

"Wait, David." The older woman, who must have been his mother, began to stand. Immediately, Sam, his father and his brother all clustered around her to help as she struggled. Her hands were red and gnarled, and it was obvious when she stepped forward that she was in pain.

Christy had seen arthritis before. Sam's mother had it worse than anyone she'd ever seen. She wanted to beg her to sit again, but it wasn't her place.

His mother waved off the men's help and shuffled to Christy. "What's your name, dear?"

Her mouth was dry. "Christina O'Malley, Mrs. Burkholder. I go by Christy."

"Christy it is." She turned to smile at Ellie. "And who is this beautiful *kind*? She has my Sam's eyes."

Ellie hung back, shy. Some of the fear drained from her eyes, though, as she looked at the sweet-faced older woman smiling down on her.

"I'm Ellie. I'm five." The child ducked her head against Sam, although she kept her eyes focused on Sam's mother.

"Eleanor Samantha." Christy gave the woman Ellie's full name, knowing all present would make the connection, just as Sam had.

"Five." David Burkholder nodded gravely. "That would mean when you were on your own the summer you were seventeen."

That was a polite way of saying he'd been thumbing his nose at his parents.

"Ellie." Sam nudged her out into the open. "This is my mother and father. Your grandparents."

Ellie was still fearful. She pointed a shaking finger at David. "Will he yell at me?"

His parents both seemed stunned by the question. Immediately, Sam knelt on one knee beside his daughter. "*Nee.* My *mamm* and *daed* are very nice people. Remember? I told you that already. They won't yell at you. In fact, I think they'll love you."

That was a bold statement.

Sam wasn't done. He gestured to the other couple in the room. "This is my brother Abram. He's your *onkel.* And that's his wife, your *aenti* Katie."

Ellie shocked them all with a wide smile at Katie. "I had an aunt before. My aunt Jo Anne." The smile faded from her face. "She'd dead now. My grandpa killed her."

All the blood drained from Christy's face. Someone helped her into a chair. In all their conversations, she'd never imagined that Ellie would have put the threads together and arrived at the same conclusion she had.

Katie's eyes became calculating. "I expect there's a story there. Levi and Lilah are coming over this afternoon. Lilah, Fannie and I are doing some baking for our quilting meeting tomorrow. I think that would be a good time for Lilah to introduce Ellie to the other children."

"*Gut* idea," Abram interjected, tossing an affectionate glance at his wife. "Then we can have an adult conversation about everything."

Sam nodded. "Sounds like the best plan."

He didn't sound thrilled, but Christy could see he wasn't as tense as he'd been when they'd arrived. He stood and nodded at his brother. "Ellie will enjoy meeting her cousins."

Ellie danced on her toes. "I have cousins?"

No one could resist smiling at her enthusiasm.

"*Jah. Onkel* Levi and *Aenti* Lilah have a four-year-old boy named Harrison and a little girl named Barbara." Sam smiled at his daughter.

Christy's heart skipped a beat. If love had a smile, it would be the one Sam showered on Ellie. How could she bear to separate them when this was done?

The sorrow gripped her with a tangible pain. How could she leave him? They were literally separated by the worlds they lived in, yet every hour, every day, this man pulled her in deeper. Soon, she'd be too emotionally invested. Her walls had failed her where Sam Burkholder was concerned.

Abram put his arm around Katie's waist. "Our *boppli* is too young to play, but you can meet our little Mary, too. When she wakes up."

"True. Christy, these are my parents, David and Fannie Burkholder. Obviously, Abram is my older brother. I've mentioned him and my oldest brother, Levi." She nodded. She'd already connected the faces with names she'd heard him speak of. "Katie, you'll be interested to know, used to be an *Englisch* police officer."

Christy started at that. Although, now that he'd said it, she realized that Katie talked somewhat differently than the others. The slightly accented speech patterns of the others was nonexistent in hers. "Had you joined the community later?"

She couldn't say why the answer was so important to her. She had no intention of becoming Amish herself. Yet, she needed to hear the answer.

Katie tilted her head. "Well…no. And yes. I grew up Amish, but I left the community for good after my parents died. I returned before I married Abram."

Before she married Abram.

Christy glanced at Sam. So far, he hadn't mentioned the part of their being married. Would he wait until his brother Levi arrived?

Apparently, yes.

Fannie fussed over Ellie for a few minutes and, before she knew it, Christy, Ellie and Sam were ushered into the kitchen for a bite to eat.

Christy hadn't realized how hungry she was until she'd bitten into the tender dumplings and homemade bread.

Ellie, who could be a picky eater, gobbled everything Fannie spooned onto her plate.

When Levi and Lilah arrived with their children, Christy stood back while Sam greeted his brother. Although Sam's face was calm, she saw the muscles bunch in his shoulders.

Sam was worried, even though he tried to give the illusion that he wasn't.

A few minutes later, she and Ellie were introduced to Levi, the oldest Burkholder brother. She recalled Sam saying that he'd left and joined the military. Levi was a quiet man, but he surprised her with his quirky sense of humor. He had an air of confidence and walked like a soldier. It wasn't until he'd put his right arm around his wife that Christy became aware it was a prosthesis. Sam had told her his brother had lost an arm. She'd forgotten until now.

Levi's wife, Lilah, was kind and sweet, with a hint of steel in her gorgeous blue eyes. She and Katie were both women that Christy would love to have as friends, if her circumstances were different.

Lilah agreed to entertain all the children while Sam and Christy acquainted his family with the whole story.

It was an uncomfortable group sitting around the kitchen table a few minutes later.

"*Sohn*, start from the beginning." David leaned his elbows on the table, his gaze intent but kind.

"You're not going to like it."

Christy cringed beside Sam.

"When I left here at seventeen," Sam said, "I went to Shipshewana."

"*Jah*. We know that." His father nodded. "You have some friends there, as I recall."

"I do. I met Christy." Hidden under the table, his hand gripped hers. For moral support, she thought.

"You had a child," Fannie murmured.

Sam hesitated. "It's worse than that."

Everyone stilled.

Christy held her breath, wincing at Sam's choice of words.

"I got married."

Christy's grip on his hand became painful. Sam held in a wince.

Levi sat forward, all the humor drained from his dark eyes. "Married? Sam, this is serious. You joined the church."

Trust Levi to go right to the important stuff. He'd always been blunt.

"We were young." Sam stared over his family's heads, choosing his words with care. "We had planned on Christy returning with me and joining the church. Then one day she disappeared."

Christy took over the narrative. "My father found me and forced me to return to his house. He threatened that he would have Sam put in jail for statutory rape. I didn't know that he couldn't do that at the time."

He listened as she told them about Jo Anne's illness and her father's shady business. When she explained how she and Ellie were kept under watch, Katie's gaze sharpened. He could almost see her cop senses going on alert.

"Why didn't you tell us?" Levi asked after her tale had ended.

Sam caught his brother's gaze. "Tell you what? By the time I realized she wasn't coming back, I also was pretty certain our whole wedding had been a fraud. We had no wedding certificate, no parental consent."

"There weren't even witnesses," Christy added. "I doubt any of it was legal."

"You'll still have to explain it to Bishop Hershberger."

"I will, Levi. I promise. But I want to make sure Christy and Ellie are safe first."

"That explains it," Abram murmured to himself, stroking his short beard.

Sam frowned at his brother. "Explains what?"

"When Katie came back, *Mamm* and *Daed* were cautioning me against getting emotionally involved with someone who wasn't Amish. You asked me if I'd marry her anyway. When I said I couldn't marry someone who wasn't Amish, you seemed sad. I wondered why you'd never walked out with a *maidel*. Now I know why."

Sam nodded. "As long as there's any doubt, I'll never marry anyone else."

ELEVEN

Hearing Sam say he'd never get married hurt. He was a man who had a lot to offer a woman. Christy was also aware that his family would not see her as an acceptable wife for Sam because she wasn't Amish, though they'd be kind and would accept Ellie as their niece and granddaughter.

She'd known this would be the case. It shouldn't have impacted her the way it did.

The soul-deep ache throbbed, but she kept her countenance neutral. Her pain would only make Sam worry. He was a strong man with an exceptionally soft heart and a core of responsibility. She couldn't allow herself to lean on him. It would cost him more than their connection already had.

Gently, she disentangled their hands under the table, feeling bereft but knowing it was for the best. Sam dropped his chin and raised an eyebrow at her. She ignored the silent question.

Katie sat across from her, a notebook and pen in her hands. "Okay, Christy. I want to go over everything that's happened to you. Everything you can recall. I have a feeling we're going to need help on this."

Christy stiffened. "The police—" The words stuck in her throat. Had she come this far only to be ensnared again?

"Relax, Christy. We have connections with the police."

She blinked. "Excuse me?"

An Amish family with ties to law enforcement?

Sam chuckled next to her. "I see that face you're making, Christy. We don't go to the police often, but it happens sometimes. I think you may even like Sergeant Nicole Dawson."

Levi leaned back. "*Jah.* I remember working with Sergeant Dawson. She was still just Officer Dawson back then. It was before Lilah and I were married. She's efficient. I'd trust her to listen and not make any rash judgments."

That was easy for them to say. She remembered the police cars surrounding her vehicle in Shipshewana. Her father and stepmother had connections, too. Ones that could make her and her daughter disappear.

And Sam. He'd been helping her for only a few days, but she knew that they had to be aware of his presence, even if they didn't know his identity.

Was it only a matter of time before her father and his cronies discovered who Sam was?

It was time for a leap of faith.

She pulled in a deep breath, repeating to herself that everything would be okay. "Fine. I'll talk with her. But only her."

Abram and Katie went to use the phone kept in the painting business office to call the police department. They returned fifteen minutes later.

Katie stepped up beside Christy. "Sergeant Dawson

isn't in today, but she'll be available first thing tomorrow. We'll go then."

She appreciated the support.

"You can leave Ellie with us," Fannie declared. "Lilah can bring Harrison and Barbara over and we'll watch the *kinder* and bake cookies."

"In the meantime," Abram said, sauntering over to lean against the counter, "Christy, I think it would be best if you and Ellie came to my *haus* this evening."

What? She hadn't been expecting that. Her heart sank. She'd be separated from Sam. Only for the night, but the idea of not having him around in these strange times made it hard to breathe.

"It'll be okay, Christy." She hadn't noticed Sam appearing at her side. "I'll see you in the morning and we'll go to the police together."

She raised her eyes to his, distressed.

He smiled, his eyes telling her not to worry. "It wouldn't be proper to have you stay in the same *haus*, Christy," David explained.

She bit her lip and nodded, unwilling to argue with Sam's father. It was settled. She and Ellie would go to Abram's house and Sam would stay here.

"I would also suggest you two dress Plain, if someone's after you," Katie declared.

Christy agreed dully, heart sore and discouraged. She didn't want to leave Sam. After spending so many years feeling caged, she'd tasted freedom. But more than that, Sam had made her feel secure.

She frowned as she considered that. Even hiding in the shed together, knowing someone was searching the barn right outside—someone who'd intended to kill her—she'd been scared, but deep inside had felt better because Sam had been with her. She trusted him completely. He was a man she could even trust with her heart.

Except, he was Amish, and she wasn't even sure what she believed. She was slowly beginning to accept that God was there. But that wasn't enough.

Plus, it didn't matter if she had feelings for Sam because her father was still out there and there were people looking for her and her daughter. Sam had introduced her to a family that was close-knit, who clearly depended on one another. She admired that. She wanted that.

She would protect it.

And that was why she had to find a way to let the man she was learning to love again go. The first time she'd left had been difficult.

This time, it would be devastating.

Christy and Ellie gathered their backpacks, said goodbye to Sam's parents and followed Abram and Katie out to their buggy.

As the buggy began to move, she looked back, her eyes snagging Sam's. He looked as lost as she felt.

Turning her gaze to the front, she said a silent prayer for the danger to pass quickly, so she and Sam could go their separate ways before any hearts were broken.

Sam watched Christy and Ellie get in Abram's buggy with mixed feelings. He was relieved that the confrontation was done—at least, the one with his family. He was also glad, though not truly surprised, that they were prepared to assist Christy in her quest to evade danger.

He hadn't been shocked when his family had agreed

to send Christy and Ellie to Abram's. In fact, he had been waiting for someone to bring up which *haus* they'd stay at.

He'd known separation was inevitable. And yet, when it came, he felt as if he'd been sucker punched. The urge to go after them took him off guard. He hadn't planned to become so attached to them. He'd fallen for Ellie quickly. And as much as he'd tried to distance himself from Christy, he hadn't succeeded. She wasn't the same girl he'd known, but he'd found the mature version of Christy almost irresistible.

His parents talked quietly after dinner was done. Everything was the same as it had been before he'd left. It was dark outside, and his *daed* had lit the kerosene lights in the *haus*. The warm glow from the woodstove in the living room combined with the lights created a cozy atmosphere. Only a few days ago, he'd sat here with his parents, almost content with his lot in life.

Now, it was as if ants were crawling under his skin. He was distracted, his mind continually returning to thoughts of Christy and Ellie. He couldn't sit still and hold a conversation.

He knew his parents were concerned, but Sam said his good-nights early. In his room, he stood in front of the window, staring up at the moon, wondering how Christy was making out at Abram's. Was she warm? Was Ellie okay? Maybe she was scared, being in a strange place.

Did Christy miss him?

He tried to shove this last thought out of his mind. Missing him was not something he wanted her to do. It wouldn't help their situation if Christy became attached to him again.

Although he had seen signs that she might have feelings for him, he had to hold off. Nothing *gut* could come of allowing their attraction to grow.

Why had *Gott* let this happen? When he'd returned to Sutter Springs six years ago, he'd been devastated, but feeling wiser. He'd reconciled with his family, had made amends with *Gott*, and had decided to dedicate his time to living the *Ordnung* and being the man *Gott* had planned for him to be.

Now, his foundation was shaking under his feet. It wasn't right to ignore Christy and Ellie when they were in danger.

Earlier, his *daed* had suggested that he leave Abram to care for them.

"*Nee, Daed.* I will take care. They are my responsibility." *My family*, he'd yearned to proclaim.

But he didn't have that right. Not while he was Amish. It was breaking his heart.

"*Gott*, what is Your plan? You know I want to serve You, to follow You. But every instinct tells me not to abandon Christy. Even though I know our marriage was probably a sham, I still feel like she is my wife. Help me."

He knew *Gott* heard his plea, but the heaviness didn't lift from his chest.

Sighing, he left his place at the window and flopped onto the bed, propping his hands beneath his head. He closed his eyes and waited for sleep to come.

An hour later, two sets of footsteps shuffled in the hall. His *daed* was assisting his *mamm* to their room. Her arthritis was getting worse, but she never complained, never talked about being in pain.

Their low voices mingled. Sam couldn't make out

any words. Not that it was hard to guess what was on their minds. They were worried about him and this new mess he'd brought to their door.

They'd always wanted him to marry and have his own family. How could he ever marry anyone else, though? *Mamm* would be sad that he didn't marry and *Daed* would be disappointed. Nothing he could do about any of that. He'd already made his choices.

Rolling onto his side, he tried to ignore the voices. Finally, they were silent. He still couldn't drift off. He spun the other way.

Was Christy able to sleep? Had Ellie sucked her thumb when she'd been put to bed? He hadn't even gotten the chance to kiss her good-night.

After what felt like hours, he drifted off to an uneasy sleep and a dream of Christy. She was in a boat and it was floating on the lake. The waves picked up, carrying the boat farther away from him. He called out to her, but she couldn't hear him. He jumped into the water and swam toward her. The waves pushed him back. The distance between them grew wider. He could barely even see her—

He bolted upright, his heart racing. It was only a dream. Christy was fine. She was with Abram. Abram would protect her. He was smart, and he was strong.

No matter how hard Sam worked to convince himself that all was well, and he could go back to sleep, it was no use. He was wide awake, adrenaline pumping through his system.

Jumping out of bed, he dressed and stuck his feet in his boots. He needed to eat, grab some *koffee* and head to Abram's *haus*. The sooner he arrived, the sooner they could leave for the police station to see

Sergeant Dawson. At this moment, all he wanted was for Christy and their daughter to be out of danger. It would surely mean they'd leave, return to the *Englisch* world, but it would be for the best.

As for him, he didn't think he'd ever be totally free of Christy, but knowing she was safe in the world would have to be enough.

TWELVE

Sam steered his mare and buggy to park in front of Abram's *haus*, arriving shortly before eight. It had been hard to wait so long before heading over, but his *daed* and *mamm* had insisted he wait. He hadn't wanted to argue with them, knowing he needed to be respectful. It hadn't been easy, though.

When he was finally able to depart, he had to hold himself back from running to the barn. He'd had to force himself to walk at a normal pace. Once the mare had been hitched to the buggy, he'd jumped up on the seat and flicked the reins to coax her into a trot.

He was in a hurry to get to Christy so they could find those after her and she and Ellie would be safe. He tried to convince himself that he had no other motives and ignored the voice in the back of his head that said he was fooling himself.

The back door flew open and a small body darted out. "Daddy!"

Laughing, he stepped down from the buggy and caught Ellie as she rushed to him. "*Gut* morning, Ellie. I almost didn't recognize you with that dress and a *kapp* on your head. What's that you're holding?"

She held up the doll. It was a typical Amish doll, dressed like a Plain girl, with no face. "This is Stella, Daddy. *Aenti* Katie gave her to me. She doesn't have any eyes or a mouth. I still like her, though."

He could listen to her chatter on for hours, he decided. She was an absolute delight. He marveled that *Gott* had given him a daughter.

His heart squeezed when he thought that someday soon she'd be leaving. How often would he be able to see her? She belonged in his life. If only...

He needed to redirect his thoughts, or he'd get depressed. "Is your *mamm* ready yet?"

"Yep." She gave an exaggerated nod. "Why do you say *mamm* instead of mommy?"

He carried her toward the *haus*. "Because that's my word for 'mommy.' My family uses a different language in our home. So, I say *daed* when talking about my father. You know, he's your *grossdawdi* in my language. And my mother—my *mamm*—you'd call *grossmammi*."

She wrinkled her nose. "That sounds strange."

A muffled laugh caught his attention. Christy opened the door to let them in. He nearly stopped when he saw her. She was lovely in a dark rose-colored dress, her brown tresses tucked under a crisp white *kapp*, only the first two inches of her hair showing. There was something beautiful about the modesty that kept a *maidel*'s hair hidden from all eyes but her husband's.

She took his breath away.

"Ellie, it's not polite to tell someone their words are strange."

Ellie pouted. "Didn't mean to be rude."

He kissed her cheek. "I know that. And now you know something new, too."

When he set her down, she clung for an extra minute before scuttling off to play.

"Abram had to leave early this morning and Barbara has a fever. I said that you and I could handle talking to the police on our own. Is that okay?" Christy said.

"Jah." He turned to address Katie, who was looking concerned. "We really don't need all of us. Did Lilah say anything else about Barbara?"

He would hate it if Levi's daughter were really sick.

"Barbara's teething, she thinks. Normal stuff. But I don't want to bring Mary over just in case."

"That's wise. We'll be fine. *Cumme*, Christy."

She thanked Katie, who swirled a black cloak around Christy's shoulders before setting a black bonnet on her head. Then she followed him out to the buggy. He had trouble not staring at her. She was beautiful.

"I'm not used to wearing two hats," she quipped. "My head's going to be toasty."

He chuckled and settled in next to her.

At the police station, he informed the receptionist that they had an appointment with Sergeant Nicole Dawson. She called for an officer to lead them to a conference room to wait for the sergeant. Sam looked around in interest. He'd never been in a police station before, although Katie had told him about the station where she used to work.

"I thought it would be busier," Christy confided. "Lots of noise and people rushing around. It seems rather anticlimactic now that we're here. Not nearly as many desks as I thought. And I always imagined a dispatcher's radio constantly going off."

He laughed. "Katie told me it's a lot more boring than people believe. She said her job had more paperwork than anything else."

"Well now, that just ruins all my expectations." She gave him an eye roll.

"Sorry. Not my intention."

The door behind them opened and they turned as a tall, slender, policewoman entered. Sam stood to greet her. Christy, however, seemed frozen in place.

Sergeant Dawson looked at her and started.

The women stared at each other for a tense moment.

"You're an officer?" The words Christy spat sounded like an accusation.

What was going on?

"I am. Sergeant Dawson. I'm sure you have questions."

Christy stood and stalked toward her. Sparks shot out of her eyes as she glared at the sergeant. "Of course I have questions. What were you doing at my house pretending to be a nurse, and where were you when my sister was killed?"

Christy clenched her fists so hard her nails bit into her palms. The pain kept the rage from exploding out of her like lava from an active volcano. She couldn't stop the little bit that leaked into her voice. This woman—this officer—had been there, pretending to be a night nurse. Christy was determined to find out why.

Poor Sam was shocked, she could see. He'd never seen her lose her temper.

"Christy, please sit. I promise I'll explain every-thing," Sergeant Dawson said.

Christy stomped back to her chair, folded her arms over her chest and jutted her chin out. "Talk. I'm lis-tening."

Sam came and sat beside her. He didn't touch her, but his presence was soothing.

Sergeant Dawson closed the door behind her and sat at the table. She offered them coffee, but Christy shook her head. She wanted answers and was impa-tient for the woman to get to the point.

"Okay. First, let me say I truly am sorry for the loss of your sister, Christy. I was on an undercover job when I met you."

Her jaw dropped. "Undercover? In my home? That's hours from here!"

Sergeant Dawson nodded. "Yes. I'm part of a state-wide task force investigating a racketeering ring that uses several businesses. There are some big names in-volved, including several government officials. Your father's business, O'Malley's Investing, Inc., is in-volved. We're sure of it. But we're not sure how deep or who is involved. I was sent to gather intel. Posing as a nurse was a good way to be in the house and ask questions. As I do have some medical knowledge, I was the best choice."

Christy was starting to settle down. She'd known her father was up to something. "Why did you dis-appear? One minute you said you'd be back, but you never returned."

"I left and made a call to the head of the task force. He informed me that my cover had been blown and I needed to leave—fast. I had no choice. Some of the information I had uncovered had hurt the racketeering operation and cost them two million dollars. My life was in danger. We never dreamed that your sister was in danger from anyone."

"One of the men said he had a score to settle. I wonder if that was it." Christy needed to move. Standing, she began to pace the room. "I wondered about you. You were very nosy, you know."

For the first time, a smile appeared on Sergeant Dawson's face. "I had to be. This is a huge investigation, and we were having trouble getting the information we needed. I can't tell you much more about the operation…" A strange look crossed the sergeant's face. Almost like pity. She appeared reluctant.

"You might as well spit it out. I can see there's something else on your mind."

"Christy," Sam chided.

She glared at him. She knew she was being rude but couldn't seem to find her balance.

"It's okay," the sergeant assured him. "She's right. There is more. It's not a pretty tale, and it's one that will upset her far more than she is now."

Christy was at her limit. "Please. No more cryptic hints. What is it? Is it something about my father? Has he done something really bad?"

Worse than murdering his own daughter? What else could they accuse him of?

"Christy, about a month ago, a couple of fishermen found a body wrapped in a tarp at the bottom of Lake Sutter. A Jane Doe. The woman had been murdered between fifteen and twenty years ago. The body was so badly decomposed, it's been impossible to identify."

Christy fell into her chair, her mind filled with static as she grew light-headed.

When she came to, she was lying on the floor. Sam was hovering over her, his face dead-white. The sergeant was on her other side.

Christy was too weak to pull herself up. "I'm fine. Sam, I'm fine," she assured him when he doubted her. "Help me up."

They both took hold of an arm and assisted her back to the table. Her stomach was roiling. Sam looked at her face then grabbed the garbage can and got it to her just in time as she lost her breakfast.

Sergeant Dawson was there a moment later with a cold, wet cloth. She handed it to Sam. He applied it gently to Christy's face until she waved him back.

Embarrassed, she flushed, but met Sergeant Dawson's eyes with a steady gaze. "You think you found my mom."

Sam's hand reached out and took hers in a gentle grasp.

"We do," the sergeant confirmed.

"And you think my father murdered her."

Hadn't she known it?

"Yeah, we do. We can't prove it, but we believe she was in the way. We found evidence that she worked briefly with the McCormicks, who are also on our watch list."

"Vanessa's family? It wouldn't surprise me." Her mother had a financial advisor. Maybe she'd found some information she shouldn't have.

"Tell me what happened the night your sister was killed," Sergeant Dawson asked, not unkindly.

It was difficult to talk about, especially hearing

about the Jane Doe they had recovered, but Christy clung tight to Sam's hand as she recounted the events of the past few days. Given the way Sergeant Dawson exclaimed when she mentioned the tracking device inside her phone, she'd managed to shock the police officer.

"I need you to take care, Christy." Sergeant Dawson leaned closer. "You've definitely got a target on your back. Would you be willing to carry a burner phone? I'd like you to be able to call for help if anything happens."

She agreed and the woman went to get one and to talk with her superior.

"Christy, I'm sorry about your mother."

She looked at Sam. Dear Sam. His face was so solemn and sincere. If only their lives had been different.

"Thanks. I think, if I'm honest with myself, I'd say I've always suspected my mother was dead. After the past few years, and especially the past few days, I can't say I'm surprised to find out my dad might have been the one who killed her."

"It's not positive it's her yet."

"True. You know, I never wanted to put your family in danger. That's another reason I never returned. I regret getting you into this mess."

"I don't." His jaw tightened. "Christy, I should have been the first one you came to. We may not really be married, but I am the father of your daughter and you know there's still a spark between us. I will always be there for you if you need me. No matter what."

She blinked back the tears. She didn't deserve the kind of devotion he showed her.

The sergeant returned. "Okay. Here's the phone."

Christy took it but had no idea what to do with it. Her clothes had no pockets. "How do I carry this?"

"Hold on."

The sergeant left and returned a few minutes later with a contraption that vaguely resembled a fanny pack. "Here, you can wear this. I know it's not in compliance with the Amish code, but then, you're not really Amish, so it should be okay."

Christy strapped it around her waist and put the phone in the pouch, feeling awkward. It would be nice having access to a phone, though.

The sergeant also had a lab technician come and scrape her cheek for a DNA analysis.

"If it's your mother, your DNA will let us know."

Five minutes later, Christy and Sam were making their way out to the buggy. After all these years, she would finally know what had become of her mother.

Would she also learn if her father was capable of cold-blooded murder?

THIRTEEN

Christy was numb. She walked out of the station without any of awareness of where she was going. Sam kept his hand lightly on her elbow. Probably to make sure she didn't walk in front of a bus by accident. Her mind swam with the enormity of all she'd heard.

"Christy, are you going to be okay?"

Sam's voice pulled her out of the darkness she'd fallen into. She shook her head, trying to rid herself of the morose mood that had enveloped her.

"I'll be fine." She tried to smile at him. The concern didn't evaporate from his face, so she guessed her smile wasn't convincing. "I'm shocked, that's all."

He nodded. "I don't blame you. Let's get home and we can plan our next move."

She had nothing to add, so she followed him silently to where the buggy was parked on the public street. Sam helped her step up into it. When he joined her, she took comfort in his solid presence at her side.

"Christy, it's okay to be upset and to feel betrayed by your father's actions. You have the right to expect your family, and especially your parents, to protect you. I don't know if you're ready to hear this, but I'm here if you need someone to vent to. You can also bring your cares to *Gott*."

She shifted so she was half facing him. "I don't know if God hears me, Sam. I've tried praying. In the last three days, particularly. I haven't seen the proof."

He nodded. "Faith is believing without the proof. I understand why you'd doubt. But I think we need to look at it from another angle."

"What angle?" Curious, she frowned at him, raising her hand to block the glare from the bright winter sun.

"You have had some very determined men after you. Men who are proficient in violence. You've even had a phone with a tracking device. All while caring for an adorable five-year-old. Yet here we are. Even if danger shows up again, *Gott* continues to help us escape."

"What if, next time, we don't get away?"

For a moment, he didn't respond. "That's possible. *Gut* people die every day. Death comes for us all. The important question isn't even about how we die. The important question is, will you be ready when you die?"

That struck her.

Would she be ready? And was she setting an example that would help her daughter to become the best person she could be?

She couldn't answer. "I'm not sure what to say to that. I do know that I'm ready to begin that conversation."

He smiled at her, hope glowing in his hazel eyes.

When they walked into Katie's kitchen a little later, they found Katie and Ellie elbow-deep in bread dough.

Ellie saw her mother and shook her head. "Mommy, I can't go yet. *Aenti* Katie needs my help. I promised I'd make bread with her."

"I didn't expect you for another hour yet," Katie said by way of explanation.

Christy smothered a grin. Sam winked at his daughter. "*Jah*, that's important work, Ellie. I think your *mamm* and I will go for a walk while you finish."

Christy let herself be steered back outside, laughing. "It's December, Sam. How far will we walk?"

He lifted his broad shoulders in a shrug, grinning. "*Jah*, but it's a pleasant December day. It's almost forty degrees out. Let's enjoy the clear roads. It's going to drop back down this evening."

They ambled down the road. She lifted her face. The warmth from the sun felt good after the traumatic morning she'd experienced. When Sam reached over and took her hand, she sighed. It couldn't last, this feeling of belonging walking next to him, but she decided to enjoy it. Just for today.

They'd been walking for fifteen minutes when the hum of a vehicle coming up the road startled her. She turned her head and the blood drained from her face as she met the eyes of the man who'd killed her sister.

Sam glanced at the driver and shoved her toward the trees. "Run!"

She didn't need to be told twice.

A shot rang out. It thunked into an ageless oak. She didn't pause as they darted around the trees. Behind her, she heard the sound of car doors slamming. Within seconds, the killers would be in the trees with them.

Ducking her head, she and Sam ran. Her side ached, but she couldn't slow down. Pressing her left hand against the complaining muscle, she kept going. She lost track of the minutes and the direction they were heading.

A second shot burst behind them. Her cloak tore.

That one was too close. They cleared the trees and were out in the open.

Sam pulled her hand and they veered to the left. A wide fenced-in field was before them. Clamoring over the fence took a few seconds, but once they'd managed it, they sprinted for the barn.

She understood Sam's thinking. If they could get behind something to shelter them, maybe they could hide. She had the phone the sergeant had given her. If they could slow down enough, she could pull it out and use it.

A single glance behind her showed Bryce and the pretend doctor were on their tail. The security guard lifted his gun again.

A bellow from the right tore through the air. She stumbled.

Bryce yelled, his eyes bulging, as the ground beneath their feet trembled. Nearby, the sound of snorting and thundering hooves rushed in their direction. She knew, without turning, what she'd see.

A large gray bull was closing in on them, nostrils flaring, head down as he charged. His angry-looking horns were long and sharp. He was heading straight for her and Sam. Before she could yell, Sam shoved her away. The bull stampeded across the exact spot she'd been standing, turned, and headed straight for Sam. Her heart was in her throat as he leaped out of the raging bull's path, hollering as a horn grazed his side.

Christy couldn't tell how badly he'd been hit. He

staggered and stumbled on his feet, his face a mask of agony, but he didn't go all the way to the ground.

She rushed to his side, forgetting for a moment about Bryce and Simms. A shout from behind her reminded her that she and Sam weren't alone in the field. Whirling, she saw Simms scrambling to get out of the bull's path. He went down. Bryce panicked and fired at the bull. The animal changed direction and headed toward the shooter.

This was her only chance. She slid her arm around Sam's waist and supported him as they fled the field.

Sam's side was on fire where the bull's horn had grazed him. Vaguely, he was cognizant of Christy's warm arm around his waist. He could tell she was trying to be careful, but her hand brushed his wound. He bit back a cry. They had no time to slow down. Between the angry bull and the two vicious men with guns who were after them, he wasn't quite sure which was more dangerous.

His shirt was sticking to his side. How much blood had he lost? It had to be a copious amount. He could feel it sliding down his ribs and spreading out along his hip.

His clothes would be ruined. The idle thought flashed through his mind and he grimaced. That was the least of his worries.

He recalled falling off a roof a few years back and catching a nail in his arm on the way down. He'd needed twelve stitches that time. The pain from that wound was nothing compared to the throbbing and burning of this one.

"Stay with me, Sam!" Christy's voice sounded like

it was coming through a tunnel. It echoed strangely in his years.

Even in his altered state, he knew he was going to lose consciousness at any moment. He had to hold off. Christy and their daughter needed him. Hadn't he just assured her that God had kept them safe on purpose?

He should pray. No prayer sprang to mind, however. The pain spreading from his side filled his mind.

Someone was breathing heavily. Harsh, gasping sounds. Hazily, he wondered if Christy had her inhaler on her, even though she was dressed in an Amish dress with no pockets. Then he realized the breathing he was hearing was his own. His lungs were burning with the need for oxygen.

He was faintly shocked. So, this was how Christy felt when she was having an asthma attack. She was so much stronger than she looked. Stronger than she even knew.

"Come on, Sam. Don't pass out on me." The harsh command jolted him out of his wandering thoughts.

"I'm trying." He sucked in another breath. *Ack*. That one hurt. "Christy... Let me go."

"Not a chance," she snapped. "Don't you even think of giving up."

"Not...giving up." He stumbled. She didn't let go, but yanked him forward. For a slender woman, she had a lot of power in her arms. "You need to get to Ellie. Get to safety. Call 9-1-1."

She ignored his words as if he hadn't spoken. Stubborn woman. All he wanted was for her to let go and get somewhere safe. The killers weren't after him. It was her they wanted.

He no longer had the breath needed to argue.

When they got beyond the field, she helped him go through the fence. Only then did she slow down.

"I don't see Bryce or Simms anywhere," she panted.

"Simms. The doctor." He remembered her telling him that she thought the man named Simms was the one who had killed her sister. "He shot at us."

He was trying to sort out the information floating around in his brain, confused by the loss of blood. He couldn't go any farther. When he sagged, she helped him lean against the base of a tree.

His eyes closed. He listened to her voice as she called 9-1-1.

If he could make it back to Abram's *haus*, she'd be safer. Ellie would be there.

Christy's hands patted his face. "Sam. Darling, open your eyes."

Darling. Hmm. He liked that. But he didn't want to open his eyes.

He had to. Christy needed him. Groaning, he forced his lids to slit open so he could see her. She wavered in front of him. He wasn't going to be able to stay conscious for long.

"Help me up." He needed to stand, to keep moving. Immediately, she was at his side, pulling him to his feet.

He looped his arm over her shoulders and they staggered to the road. They'd only gone a few feet when sirens blared through the air. It could have been seconds or minutes later when he opened his eyes again and found himself on a stretcher.

"Christy."

A stranger popped into his view. "Mr. Burkholder,

the police took your wife to your brother's house to check on your daughter. She'll join you at the hospital."

His wife. He should correct the man. He didn't, though.

Christy was safe.

Ellie was safe.

He allowed his eyes to shut. He felt a needle penetrate his arm and, within moments, found himself being pulled into darkness.

FOURTEEN

Christy sat in the front seat of the police cruiser, her hands clenched into tight fists. Sam had to be all right. She bit her bottom lip, trying to hold tears and screams at bay. When she looked down, she was startled to see there was blood on her hands.

Sam's blood.

She didn't know what she would do if anything happened to him. He'd only been back in their lives for four days, but he was more important to her now than he had ever been. Regardless of whether or not they could ever be together, whether they could ever truly be husband and wife, she knew that she loved him.

Maybe she always had.

And now, because of her, he was fighting for his life. He was also alone at the hospital. She had to go to him. But not before she made sure Ellie was safe.

Her whole body went cold. What if Bryce and Simms had gone to Abram's house first? What if they had gotten to Katie and Ellie? Her legs bounced up and down as she tried to stem the anxiety jittering through her body.

"We'll be there in just a moment, miss." The officer

stopped talking as a call came in on the radio. "I won't be able to stay. I have to answer this call. One of the men who had chased you got away and has been spotted."

She understood. "I'll find my way to the hospital. Go after him."

Vaguely, she wondered if it was Bryce or Simms.

"You'll be okay, then?"

She nodded at the officer sitting beside her. He was kind, but he could have no idea of the terror and guilt running through her. This was all her fault. If she hadn't involved Sam…

Then what? She settled as peace flooded through her soul until she felt saturated with it. She had gone to Sam because he was the only one she had. He had made the choice to help them, and she knew that he didn't regret it.

When the cruiser stopped in front of Abram's house, Christy flung the door open and bolted from the vehicle. She flew toward the house and entered, letting the door bang shut behind her. Ellie and Katie were still in the kitchen. They looked up and smiled as she entered. Katie's smile dropped instantly. Her eyes sharp as she scanned Christy, taking in the blood-stained dress.

"Where's Sam?"

She has cop's eyes.

Christy jerked her head in Ellie's direction. Katie nodded.

"Honey, Mommy needs to talk with *Aenti* Katie for a minute. Why don't you take your new dolly and go into the other room?"

Ellie smiled at her mother and happily complied.

Christy waited until she was alone with Katie before

she started explaining. "The men who were chasing me around found us. We ran through the field to escape, but there was a bull there." Katie's hands flew to her mouth and her eyes flared wide. Christy turned away so she could continue her explanation without breaking down. "Sam was gored, but I don't know how badly. He was able to walk a little bit. I called 9-1-1. He's on his way to the hospital."

"You need to go. I heard the car leave." Katie's eyebrows lifted.

"The officer is going back to search for Bryce—or Simms. One of them got away."

Katie walked over and surprised Christy with a hug. "Abram will be here soon. When he gets home, you can have him take you to the hospital. I'll stay with Ellie. No one will get to her."

When Abram returned to the house, it only took a few minutes before he was running out to hitch the horse to the buggy again. Christy had feared he would blame her, but there was nothing but concern for her and his brother in his kind gaze.

As they were getting ready to leave, Christy called Ellie to her side. "Honey, your daddy's been hurt in an accident. He's at the hospital. I'm going to go stay with him for a bit. Be a good girl for Mommy and stay with *Aenti* Katie, okay?"

The little girl's eyes filled with tears. "Mommy, I don't want Daddy to be hurt. I want Daddy to be here with me."

Christy couldn't speak. She pulled the little girl into her arms and held her tight for a moment until Ellie wiggled to get free.

"Love you, Mommy!" Ellie dashed out of the room.

Less than a minute later, she was back, her Amish doll in her arms. "Take Stella with you. She'll make you feel better if you get sad."

Touched, Christy gently took the doll from her daughter. She knew how much the toy meant to her. "Sweetie, I'll take very good care of Stella. And, you're right. She'll help me not be sad."

Satisfied that she'd helped her mommy, Ellie smiled and nodded. "I'll help *Aenti* Katie until you get back with Daddy."

She caught her daughter close in another hug and kissed her soft cheek. Turning to Katie, she embraced her, too. "Thank you. For everything," she whispered.

"Go." Katie smiled. "We'll be waiting when you get back."

Christy whirled away and raced out the door, Ellie's rag doll clasped tightly in her arm. Abram was waiting. Once she was seated next to him, he flicked the reins and the horse started off. She grabbed the seat as she swayed when the buggy jolted.

"How long will it take us to get to the hospital?"

"It's going to be thirty minutes or so."

She wanted to scream. That seemed such a long time. But she held her complaint in. She knew that if they'd called for a driver, it could have taken half an hour or longer just for the car to arrive. The waiting would have driven her up the walls. At least this way, they were doing something.

Christy gazed with unseeing eyes at the snow-covered landscape they passed. There was a slight bump as the buggy left the graveled back road and transitioned to the paved road. The traffic was thicker. Several vehicles moved around them to pass. Abram didn't seem to mind, but each time a car passed, she cringed, half expecting to see a gun pointing out of a window at her.

She breathed in deep.

At a light, Abram pulled on the reins to stop the buggy. She looked around, noticing the Christmas displays surrounding them. The people in Sutter Springs had a lighter hand in decorating than Vanessa had. These tasteful displays were cheerful without being overdone. As the light changed, Abram clicked the reins, and the horse resumed its pace.

The hospital was smaller than the one near her house, which wasn't surprising. Abram pulled the buggy in under the white cement carport supported by large pillars to the hospital entrance. It reminded her of the columns from ancient Greek architecture.

"You go in," Abram said. "I'll park and join you. Find out where he is and what his condition is."

She started to get down, but paused. "Will they tell me? Usually, they only tell family."

A strange smile quirked his lips. "Tell them you're his wife."

Her mouth dropped open as he reined the horse to move.

His wife. How she wished it were true. But she didn't know for a fact that their marriage wasn't legal, so she'd use that while she could.

Inside the hospital, the emergency room waiting area was teeming with people either anticipating news or awaiting examination. She pulled her cloak tighter around herself and approached the reception desk.

"My...my husband was brought in. Sam Burkholder. He was gored by a bull." She left out the part about being chased by Bryce and Simms, as none of that was important.

The nurse gave her a sympathetic glance. "Of course, dear. He's still in the treatment area." She handed her a clipboard. "Go sit over there and fill this out. Someone will be with you when there's news."

Unsure, Christy hesitated at the entrance to the waiting area. There were three empty chairs on the far wall. She headed in that direction, taking care not to meet anyone's eyes. She had a silly feeling that if she did, someone would realize what a fraud she was and that she wasn't really Amish.

Sitting, she took a look at the paperwork. How was she supposed to fill this out? She didn't even know his house number. When Abram strode in a moment later and lowered himself into the chair beside hers, she handed him the clipboard without a word.

He smirked and began to fill out all the necessary information.

"Christy!" She looked up to see Sergeant Dawson approaching. "I heard the call when it came in. Any news?"

She shook her head. "Nothing yet."

"I need to talk with the officer who responded to the call. I'll stop by in a bit to touch base with you after I know more."

Christy nodded and watched her move off.

Through the next forty-five minutes, the occupants in the waiting area changed as people came and left. Her back began to ache from sitting so long in the hard plastic chairs.

"They really should invest in cushions."

Abram chuckled at her muttered comment.

She sat straighter when a doctor appeared and strode their way. Nudging Abram, he looked up and stood. The doctor introduced himself, but she missed the name because her heart was thudding too loudly in her ears.

"Your husband was fortunate. The bull's horn missed all his internal organs. We've stopped the bleeding and he's been given stitches. He's also been given morphine for the pain. As soon as it wears off and he's awake, he can leave. I'll leave instructions with him on how to care for the wound."

"Can we go in and sit with him?"

"Yes. He's been moved to a room because we needed all the bays in the emergency area. Take the elevator to the second floor, turn left, and he'll be the third door on the right." The doctor gave them the room number and left.

They went to the elevator and Abram pressed the button for the second floor. When the door finally opened, they got out and started toward the door.

Her stomach lurched. Seeing a restroom, she slowed and pointed. "I'll be there in a moment."

Abram nodded and she ran to the restroom. Once inside, she set the black bonnet on the edge of the sink and twisted the cold water knob on the faucet. She dipped her hands into the water. Pressing her damp palms to her cheeks, she tried to steady her breathing. Sam was fine. He would recover.

Once her stomach settled down and her pulse slowed, she picked up the bonnet and left the restroom.

As she turned to the left, a hard hand grabbed her right elbow.

Annoyed, she frowned and spun.

Her heart sank as she came face-to-face with the one man responsible for all the misery in her life.

Her father.

"Christina." That one word had her trembling from head to foot. "Don't make a fuss. Don't scream or try to call for help. If you come with me, Ellie and your boyfriend will be left alone."

He knew about Sam. He probably also knew where Ellie was. She had to protect them. She had no choice but to go with him.

"Please," she begged, refusing to call him *father* or *dad*. He wasn't really a father. Not like Sam was to Ellie. "Let me say goodbye."

He scoffed. "And give you time to warn him."

"His brother is with him. He knows I'm here. If I don't give him some kind of excuse, he'll come looking for me. I don't want him hurt—or Ellie, or Sam."

He glared at her, but finally relented. "I'll be standing right here. If you try anything, I'll hear it."

Sam was floating. He was warm and comfortable.

After a few moments, he became aware of noises around him. Voices were humming, but he couldn't make out the words. He heard Abram's low rumble, and a higher voice, feminine.

He didn't hear the one voice he wanted to hear, though. Where was Christy? His mind was sluggish. Something had happened, something he should know. As awareness slowly filtered in, the medication-induced haze dimmed. He grimaced. His side began to throb.

A bull. He'd been stabbed by a bull's horn. Two men had chased him and Christy. They'd had guns.

His eyes popped open. He and Christy had been walking, and Bryce and Simms had chased them into the field. The memory of the gray bull charging directly at Christy filled his mind. He remembered shoving her out of the way. He recalled her helping him move. Everything else was a blur.

Had Bryce and Simms gotten away?

Had Christy made it to safety?

"Sam! You're awake." Abram's grinning face appeared in his line of vision. Surely, Abram wouldn't be grinning like that if Christy were injured.

"Where's Christy? And Ellie? Abram, where are my wife and daughter?"

Abram's grin faded. "Sam, they're fine. Christy stopped in the restroom. I think she needed a minute to regain her composure." He hesitated. "Is it really a *gut* idea to keep thinking of her as your wife? I told her to say she was so that she could see you. But, Sam, she's not Amish."

"*Jah.* I know this." His jaw clenched. He was well aware of how things stood between them. "Understand this, Abram. In my mind, in my heart, she is my wife. When we went through that ceremony six years ago, both of us said our vows in *gut* faith, believing them to be true. Even if we found out that we were not married in truth, I would want no other than she. I will take no other wife than Christy. If that means I live out my life alone, I accept that. I have no alternative. Could you replace Katie?"

Abram sighed and shook his head. "*Nee.* I couldn't. I understand what you're feeling. Remember, I was in love with Katie when she disappeared years ago."

Sam narrowed his gaze on his brother. "*Jah.* I remember. You had planned on marrying her when you were young. For a bit, though, I thought you'd marry Linda."

"You didn't approve." It wasn't a question.

"*Nee*. I knew you didn't love her. It was clear to anyone who saw you together."

"Just as it's clear you love Christy."

He would never deny it again.

Sam's eyelids were growing heavy. He was more tired than he could ever recall being in his life.

"I'll be back," Abram told him.

He was barely aware of his brother slipping out of the room. He'd just close his eyes and rest until he came back.

He had no idea how long Abram had been gone when he became aware of a familiar fragrance. "Christy."

"Sam, wake up."

He pulled his heavy lids open, and she was there. Her face was a little pale.

"Christy, what—?"

"No time. I have to go." She leaned forward to kiss him. Her lips grazed his then feathered over his cheek to his ear. "My dad's here."

He'd barely heard the words she'd breathed in his ear before she was gone. He tried to call her back, but his eyelids refused to remain open any longer.

Sam jerked awake.

Christy! He sat quickly upright in the bed. The room spun.

"Whoa, Sam, steady." Abram pushed him down.

"How long have I been asleep?" He searched his

brother's face. Abram was disturbed about something. His normally robust complexion was pale. Sam knew something was wrong, and he suspected Christy was at the heart of it.

"Abram, where is my wife?"

Please, Gott, *let this all have been a dream.*

Abram shook his head. "I don't know. I expected her to be here when I came back, but she wasn't. That was half an hour ago."

Frantically, Sam straightened, pushing away his brother's hands when Abram tried to stop him. "She was here. Christy was here, but I was half-asleep. She came in, kissed me and said goodbye. And then she whispered her dad was here."

Abram reared back in horror. "Hold on! Sergeant Dawson is in the hospital. She is also looking for Christy. Let me go get her."

Abram left the room, but Sam wasn't about to sit still and wait for him to return. Throwing back the covers keeping him warm, he sat on the edge of the bed and looked around him. His shirt was missing, but his boots and other items were still viable. He stood, removed the hospital gown, yanked on his remaining clothes, and sealed his coat across his chest so that he was decent. He was shoving his feet into his boots just as Abram and the police sergeant ran into the room.

"Sam! What's this I hear? Was Christy taken by her father?"

He nodded. "*Jah.* That's exactly what happened. I don't know what he wants or why he let her come in to see me."

"My guess is he wants to find out what she knows."

Sam stared at Sergeant Dawson. "And once he's done that?"

He saw the answer in the set of her lips and the sorrow in her eyes.

He finished the thought she didn't want to say.

"He plans to kill her."

FIFTEEN

Sam left the hospital room with his brother and Sergeant Dawson. He pressed his hand to his bandaged side, determined to ignore the way it ached and throbbed. It was nothing when compared to the agony in his heart and soul caused by his missing wife. He couldn't bring himself to imagine the possibility that he might never see her again. Instead, he promised himself that he would not rest until she was found safe and sound. An unending litany of prayer tumbled inside him, pleading for her safety.

In the elevator, he listened as Sergeant Dawson relayed pertinent details to someone on the receiving end of her phone call. She was giving the officer, he presumed, a detailed description of Christy, right down to the color of the clothes she'd been wearing.

"She's wearing a rose-colored dress, brown boots, a dark cloak and a black bonnet over a white bonnet."

Prayer kapp. *It's called a prayer* kapp.

He didn't interrupt. He might be frustrated, but he wasn't about to take it out on those trying to help him.

"She's about five-six, has dark brown hair, brown eyes… Sam?" He looked over at the sergeant. When she pointed to her hair, he held a hand about an inch below his shoulder. She nodded. "If her hair's not bound, it's about shoulder length… Right. No tattoos or other marks that would help identify her." She quirked her brow at Sam as she said this.

He shook his head. *Nee.* There were none that he could remember.

The way she described Christy, she could have been one of hundreds of women. How were they supposed to find her with such superficial descriptions?

"Look up her driver's license," the sergeant continued. "While she's dressed in Amish clothes now, her picture should be recent enough to still match… I saw her just this morning. So, if necessary, I can look to see if she's changed a substantial amount… I doubt we'll need the aid of our sketch artist."

The elevator door swished open and the three of them filed out.

An officer met them at the reception desk. He was young, around Sam's age, and appeared miserable.

"Hendricks. Do you have something for me?" Sergeant Dawson demanded.

"Yes, ma'am." The young officer's gaze slid past his superior officer's and landed on Sam and Abram. He hesitated, but apparently decided that if she didn't mind him making a report in front of civilians, he wouldn't worry about it, either.

"Ma'am, I dropped the missing woman off at her family's home." He recited Abram's address. "Should I have stayed? Is this my fault?"

Sam could appreciate the young man's angst. He often felt guilty himself. Especially lately. And it all seemed to be related to Christy. *Stop! Focus on finding her.*

"You did the right thing, Hendricks. The woman came to the hospital with family, and I myself saw her here. None of us noticed when she went absent. Nor did any of us notice that her father was present. Let's make a thorough search. I want the security tapes. I've already contacted a judge to get the warrant. Let's find her."

Sam agreed with his whole heart. "Sergeant Dawson, what about the other men that chased us in the field today? I don't know either man's full name. Christy called them Bryce and Simms."

She motioned for the group to move away from the desk. No doubt she didn't want any outside ears overhearing. "I meant to tell you earlier when I saw you. Bryce Walters was spotted in town. He was chased, but managed to evade arrest. We are still searching for him and will continue until he is caught. The other man, the one you called Simms, is actually known as Tyson Simpson. He was pronounced dead this afternoon."

"Did the bull kill him?" Sam wondered aloud.

"The bull had knocked him down but, actually, his partner shot him. Probably because Simpson's leg was broken. He was a liability."

What kind of people were these? One horror after another. He shuddered. His Christy was at their mercy.

Sam and Abram walked out into the parking lot with Sergeant Dawson. Abram's buggy was the only buggy in sight.

Sam started to turn away, but something caught his eye. Something small and black and familiar.

"Wait a minute." He hurried off. When Abram and

the sergeant called his name, he held up a hand, telling them to hold on.

Walking over to the buggy, he bent to retrieve a black bonnet from the ground. Standing, he peered inside the buggy. Ellie's little doll was sitting on the bench, as if waiting for them to come and get her. He swallowed. How would he explain to his little girl that her mommy was gone?

When he turned back, his eyes were dry but his jaw was tense, his throat tight. He would bring her home.

Holding his empty hand to his bandaged side, he jogged over to join the others, who had started his way. "She dropped her bonnet next to the buggy. That couldn't have been accidental."

"So we know she came out here to get into a vehicle. We'll get the security feed and then we'll have more information." Sergeant Dawson continued to give more instructions to Officer Hendricks.

Sam was ready to jump out of his skin. He could hardly stand still, waiting for the police to complete their investigation. Christy was missing. What's more, they knew the identity of the man who had abducted her. What were they moving so slow for?

An hour and a half later, someone had loaned him a shirt and he sat with Sergeant Dawson and Abram as she showed them the video feed. The officers had already conferenced, but she was gracious enough to bring them in on the investigation.

"The man walking beside Christy has been positively identified as Patrick O'Malley," she told them. Sam's hands curled into fists as they watched that man march beside her, holding her elbow. It might have seemed a gentlemanly gesture, a man ensuring a woman didn't slip on the icy parking lot, but he knew better. Her father was making sure she didn't run.

They watched as the pair walked past the buggy and she turned to look inside. Sam knew the moment Christy's eyes saw the doll. She dropped the hat in front of the buggy, probably to show where they were heading.

Patrick opened a car door and she got in. She didn't fight. Didn't try to escape.

"Why didn't she try to run?" Abram queried.

"Because of Ellie." All eyes rounded on Sam. "That's her father. He knows what buttons to push, what motivates her. There is nothing he could threaten her with that would get her cooperation faster than threats to her daughter."

And maybe threats to him, as well. He remembered hearing Christy calling him and Ellie her only family.

"Perhaps you're right."

Suddenly, he straightened, stricken. "My daughter. And my sister-in-law might be in danger!"

Before he could get worked up, Abram put a hand on his arm. "*Alles ist gut*, Sam."

"How do you know all is well?" He wanted to believe his brother but needed some further reassurance.

"I was worried myself, so Sergeant Dawson sent an officer to my *haus*. He's still there, keeping watch over our family."

Sam allowed himself to relax in his chair. Ellie was fine. Patrick O'Malley wouldn't get to her, and neither would any of his hired hitmen or employees. Both terms probably applied. "What do we do now?"

"We've been watching the interstates for his car," the sergeant told him. "Which, I'll admit, is most likely a lost cause. A man of his experience has no doubt already ditched his vehicle. I have contacted the police department near his residence outside of Columbus. Even as we speak, they're searching the property. And the business offices. Every place that Patrick O'Malley lives or does business of any kind will be searched. And that includes places his wife frequents."

There was a slight sneer in her voice when she talked of Vanessa. He recalled that she'd worked undercover as a nurse at the O'Malley home. She had experience with the woman and was clearly not a fan.

The police were taking Christy's disappearance seriously. He only hoped all their efforts were enough.

Christy hadn't fought when her father had grabbed her elbow and shoved her toward the car. She'd walked beside him, aware that there was a gun in his pocket. There was no longer a doubt that he'd use it if he had to. Her goal was to get him as far from her family as she could.

When she'd seen Abram's buggy, her heart had leaped into her throat. She hadn't been able to keep herself from looking inside. Ellie's doll.

Her baby. Would she never see her again?

"Keep moving." Her dad had shoved her. Pretending to trip, she'd deliberately dropped her bonnet, hoping anyone who saw would realize they'd come that way.

It was all she could do.

"If you scream, or run, our deal's off. I will go to the Amish man's house and get Ellie, no matter who tries to stop me."

She hadn't resisted and had ducked into the car.

Christy now watched as the miles speed by. She had

nothing to say to the man at her side, even if he was her father. Patrick O'Malley, as far as she was concerned, had ceased to be her father when she was six years old.

She was slowly becoming more certain that he had been responsible for her mother's death seventeen years earlier and her sister's death last week. She was done giving him the benefit of a doubt. Even if he hadn't been the one to actually murder the two women of her childhood family, he was involved.

To what extent, she no longer cared.

All she wanted was Ellie and Sam. However, she was pretty sure she was on her way to her own death. As sad and scared as she was, she also had a small kernel of gratitude growing in her heart that her daughter was safe, and would be raised by a father, grandparents, and aunts and uncles who loved her. Ellie would be cherished and protected.

With that, she had to be content.

Suddenly, she frowned. They weren't heading toward Columbus. She'd assumed when she'd gotten into the vehicle that her father would take her home. She'd been wrong. Where were they heading?

When the car turned off the interstate, she watched the signs and the mile markers. It took her a while, but she finally figured it out.

"We're going to Grandpa Marshal's farm." Her mother's father had left his property to their mother. However, after she'd disappeared, he had changed his will to leave it to Jo Anne. Her father had taken over the care of the property when Jo Anne had become too sick to manage it, although it remained in her name.

He laughed softly. "I'm surprised it took you this long to figure it out. Our house will be the first place anyone will search for you." He speared her with a hooded glance. "I don't intend for you to be found so easily."

He had a good point. Not many people knew the property even existed.

Any hope she had for rescue dissolved.

Turning her face away from him, Christy stared out the window. Her eyes were dry. She had no more tears to cry.

It was late afternoon by the time they arrived. Her father pulled up the long driveway. While the farm itself was dark, the house on the property next door exploded with Christmas lights. The yard was filled with figurines, blown-up Christmas snowmen and candy canes. There were moving figurines in the windows and a sleigh on the roof. She wondered idly what their monthly electric bill was like.

In contrast, their farm appeared to be dead.

Her father pulled her from the car and led her into the house. They walked through the enclosed porch, which her grandfather had always called the Florida room, and straight to the door that led to the basement.

Christy shuddered as her father open the door.

"Hurry up! We don't have much time." He pointed an imperious finger at the stairs. His brow lowered when she didn't immediately follow his instructions.

Confused, she hung back. All her life, she and Jo Anne had enjoyed playing in the basement. To have it play a part in this horrible drama seemed somehow obscene. Even the storm brewing on her father's face failed to convince her to obey him.

"If you have any hope of surviving the night, I suggest you do as I tell you. Now." His voice had taken on the low rumble of a growl.

This was it.

She started to take the first step when the sound of wheels on the driveway changed the plan. Her father grabbed her arm and propelled her down the steps. She would have tripped and fallen on her face if he hadn't pulled her upright before she'd landed. He didn't stop once they reached the bottom. Instead, he dragged her around the corner and pushed open the door to what she and her sister had always referred to as the bomb shelter.

It was a small room, completely made of cement. Ceiling-high shelves had been built against two of the four walls. The one shelf was filled with canned goods and bottled water. The shelf on the other wall was filled with camping supplies and other outdoor equipment. A third wall was barren except for the narrow cot placed against it. The outside wall slanted inward. At the top were the cellar doors to the outside.

"I've chained the doors shut, so you won't be able to escape," her father told her. "And don't waste your time shouting."

Before she could do anything, he backed out of the room and slammed the door shut. She rushed at it, but it was sealed shut and bolted. Hot tears of anger tracked down her cheeks. The monster had locked her into a veritable prison. Not only could she not get through the door to the outside, the inside walls and door were soundproof. No matter how much she yelled, no one inside the basement or upstairs would hear her.

She had food and water, though. And even a sleeping bag.

Why had her father spared her life? What torture was he planning?

She also wondered who had pulled in to make him react so fiercely. Maybe the police had found her.

She felt hope kindle, but after sitting for several long minutes, the small spark was extinguished.

Her father had tossed the burner phone when he'd kidnapped her, so even if she had service in this basement, which was unlikely, she was unable to call anyone.

Her only hope was Sam and Sergeant Dawson.

No. She was wrong.

She had someone else who was listening. Someone who may be willing to help.

Sinking onto the cold cement floor, Christy closed her eyes and bowed her head. At first the words wouldn't come. She was overwhelmed; it was hard to focus and form a coherent prayer. *Start simple. Make it an honest plea.*

Lord, if You're listening, protect Sam and Ellie. And if it is Your will, I'd appreciate it if You'd send someone to rescue me.

SIXTEEN

Saturday evening, Sam and Abram returned home without hearing any news of what had become of Christy. When Sam got down off the buggy at his brother's haus, he felt as if he'd aged ten years.

Everything ached. Physically, his side was hurting, although he refused to take more medication. If he hadn't been under the influence of the morphine, he might have been able to react faster when Christy had come to him. She had told him who was taking her and, through no fault of his own, he'd failed her.

He'd let her father steal her from him again.

Even worse than the physical pain, however, was the soul-deep ache that went with missing the one woman who'd become his world. Was she cold? Hurting?

He refused to consider that she might be dead.

Abram wouldn't meet his eyes. His brother was likely already thinking that. Sam couldn't lose hope yet. Not until they'd exhausted every possibility, looked in every nook and cranny, would he give up hope that his Christy was still alive. He knew that she couldn't be his, but she'd be alive.

Dear Gott. *Please, Lord. I can give her up if I have to. Just bring her home safe.*

Sam walked into the kitchen. Ellie saw him and gasped, running to get a hug. Pulling her into his embrace, he held her close, burying his face in the side of her *kapp*. He couldn't release her until the tremors that shook his frame ebbed.

"Daddy? Daddy!" Her little fingers poked at his shoulders. Finally, he was in control and raised his face to her.

"Hey, Ellie. Did you have a *gut* day?" He nearly winced at the foolish question. But she didn't know. All the way here, he'd debated how much to tell her. He was not staying the night, but she was going to stay here so he would be free to continue working with the police in the morning.

"Daddy, why are you sad?"

Kinder saw so much more than adults thought they did.

"I'm tired, Ellie. You're going to stay here tonight, okay? I have to leave early in the morning, and your *aenti* Katie said you were a big help today, ain't so?"

Ellie nodded, pleased. Then a shadow fell over her face. "Where's Mommy?"

Abram and Katie stilled. He looked up at them, pleading for help. The pain was almost too much. Katie's eyes swam in her tears, but she didn't let them fall. He'd been aware on some level of Abram taking her to the next room to talk.

"Ellie, Mommy can't come over tonight, okay? She loves you, but she had to do something." Not of her own free will, either. He made sure he wasn't speaking a lie. She'd had enough lies in her life. If they didn't find Christy tomorrow, he'd have to tell her.

The parallel between her life and Christy's suddenly struck him like a lightning bolt. Christy had only been a few months older than Ellie when her mother had disappeared. Then today—

Nee! He wouldn't think about it. She was alive. She had to be.

He didn't remember the drive back to his parents' *haus*, or what he'd told his *mamm* and *daed*.

All he could do was fall into his bed, knowing he'd get no sleep that night. He didn't plan on sleeping. He would be up, keeping watch with *Gott* all night, praying his Christy home.

At 5:00 a.m., Sam woke up. He'd somehow dozed off around four. He knew trying to go back to sleep was useless, so he went to the kitchen, doing his best to be quiet. He stoked the fire in the woodstove. Once the fire was going, he set about brewing a pot of *koffee*. He'd need it.

A few minutes later, his *daed* joined him. He gave his father a nod but didn't trust himself to speak. For a few minutes, the two men sat silently, sipping their *koffee*.

David Burkholder cleared his throat. "*Sohn*, is there anything I can do to help?"

Sam looked at his father, a man who'd seen his own share of sorrow. Sam hadn't thought about the sister who'd died of leukemia years before, but he did now. His father had stood by and watched his *kind* sicken and die. Then he'd watched another *sohn* leave the church and return a broken man. Even now, David watched his wife, a woman he'd been married to for close to thirty years, grow weak with pain. He hadn't been able to do anything about any of those situations.

"How do you do it, *Daed*?" he blurted. "How do

you stand by and watch those you love get hurt, or die? How do you stay strong?" It was a cry from his heart.

His *daed* sighed. "I wish I could tell you what you want to hear. All I can tell you is to trust *Gott*'s plan. His plan may not be easy, and sometimes you'll want to scream at Him. But His way is best and always right."

Sam lifted his head and stared at his *daed*, shocked that his strict father would admit to having ever been angry at *Gott*.

"Daed." He didn't know what else to say.

David stood and rounded the table. "Trust, Sam. And believe. I know you will do the right thing. Your *mamm* and I are here for you."

Resolved, Sam rose and nodded at his father, knowing what he had to do.

Hitching the buggy, he headed for the police station. He wasn't sure if Sergeant Dawson would be there.

She was. When she saw him, her forehead creased in surprise, but she didn't protest. Instead, she waved him over and led him into the conference room. "We have no leads, Sam," she told him.

His shoulders drooped as she continued. "The house in Columbus has been searched. As have all Patrick's properties. There's been no sign of him. Or of Bryce Walters, his security guard."

Sam frowned, a memory nudging the corner of his mind. A conversation he'd once had with Christy years ago. "Did you check the farm?"

The sergeant had been lowering herself into a chair. At his words, she stood straight and stared at him. "Farm? Explain."

A spark of hope reignited.

"Christy's mom's parents had a farm. They left it to Jo Anne."

She ran to the hall and yelled for Officer Hendricks. When the young officer arrived, she pointed at Sam. "Tell us everything you know about this farm."

Real excitement simmered in the air. He could taste it. They hadn't know about the place, which meant they hadn't searched it. Could it be?

Sergeant Dawson left the room after he'd relayed what he remembered about the farm's location. When she returned about ten minutes later, she'd grabbed a jacket and was buckling on her gun belt.

"I have done a search of the streetlight cameras. Christy's dad's not as clever as I thought. His car was spotted last night, headed in the right direction for the farm. We'll head there. I'm assuming that you're coming with me?"

He nodded. "I thought I'd have to hide in your car."

She rolled her eyes. "I considered doing it without you. But I remember the fight we had when we tried to leave Levi behind when Lilah was in trouble. Since you and Christy are already married, I don't think I'd have much success with that."

Sam didn't argue, just followed her out to her cruiser. Officer Hendricks was already behind the wheel of the vehicle next to theirs.

"Wouldn't it be more efficient for you guys to go in one cruiser?"

"Not really." She backed out of her space and spun from the lot, hitting the button to turn on the lights. The strobes splashed splotches of blue and red on the road and on the snow. Cars pulled over to the side to allow them access. "If we have to separate and chase different suspects, we'll both need to have a car."

He hadn't considered that. His heart thudded in his chest and the adrenaline surged.

Hold on, Christy. We're coming for you.

Sam was glad the sergeant was using the lights. They sliced through the traffic smoothly and avoided stopping at red lights. He didn't know how long it might normally take to arrive at the farm, but he could tell even on the interstate that they were leaving the other vehicles in the dust.

He wasn't about to complain.

Sergeant Dawson turned off the lights as they approached the farm property. "We don't want to let O'Malley know we're on to him. We'll pull into the lot behind the farm and walk through the backyard."

He nodded.

She speared him with a glance. "I don't have to tell you to stay out of the way."

He agreed. Anything to go with them.

She pinned him with her eyes, but finally decided to trust him.

Two local police cruisers pulled up beside them. Sam also saw a man, wearing an FBI jacket, walking around. His eyes wide, Sam looked at Sergeant Dawson. She shook her head, frowning. He took that to mean she had no idea why the FBI was there.

The group made their way silently on foot to the front of the *haus*. There were three vehicles in the driveway. Sam recognized the first car as the one Christy had gotten into. He pointed to it. Sergeant Dawson nodded. She'd seen it, too.

Christy was here.

The police and the FBI agent swarmed the *haus*, knocking in the door and rushing in. There was shouting and a few shots fired before everything quieted down.

Officer Hendricks was given the job to keep watch outside. He and Sam wandered around to the far side of the *haus*. Sam saw a pair of orange cellar doors. Curious, he stepped closer.

What was that? Leaning in, he caught his breath. Was that Christy shouting? Pointing at the doors, Officer Hendricks caught on. Using his gun, he shot the lock off and pulled the chain free.

Sam wrenched the doors open.

Christy, pale and dirty, dried tear tracks on her beautiful cheeks, stared up at him.

Sam was staring down at her. She blinked. Was she dreaming? She attempted to stand. She'd been cold for so long, her legs had stiffened and gone numb. Pins and needles raced along her legs when she moved them.

Sam didn't just walk down the cellar steps. He jumped over them and caught her up in a hug.

"Are you all right? Did he hurt you?" His words tumbled over each other as he held her away from him and examined her.

Christy laughed. It was little more than an exhausted chuckle. "He put me in here and locked me in. It's soundproof—at least, the walls inside are—so I have no idea what was happening."

"I'm glad the cellar door wasn't soundproofed. That's how we found you. I heard you."

He helped her up through the orange doors. She turned her head away from the bright light. It took a moment for her eyes to adjust. When they did, she got a good look at Sam's face. It was haggard. His smile was bright and happy, but she could see that he had not slept much more than she had the night before.

"It looks like it was a rough night for both of us," she joked. She couldn't help it. Seeing him again made her giddy.

His smile faltered as his gaze darkened. Slowly, he brought his head down and kissed her. It was a gentle kiss, little more than a soft caress, but it told her how very much he'd missed her and had feared for her.

"I wouldn't let myself believe you weren't alive. I couldn't."

"I'm happy you didn't. I wasn't so sure I'd make it."

He looped his arm around her waist. She'd been cold for so many hours, she craved the heat and leaned against him, shivering. He stepped away and she immediately missed his touch. He was back a second later, placing his coat around her shoulders, over her cloak.

"Sam, no, you'll be cold." It was starting to snow. Light, fluffy snowflakes. The kind that was perfect for Christmastime.

"*Ack*. I'm well. You're like an ice cube, Christy. We need to get you warm."

"I was in that bomb shelter all night," she admitted, sighing as she started to feel a little warmer. At least she'd stopped shaking so hard.

A yell from behind them broke off any further conversation. Whirling, she was confronted by her father, a gun raised in his hand.

Without thinking, she grabbed on to Sam, holding him tight. He moved, blocking her father's access to her, making himself the target.

The gun barked and they both jumped.

A cry beyond them had her shoving at Sam in confusion. "Are you hurt?" She couldn't see any blood.

He shook his head and pointed. Turning, she saw Bryce lying on the ground, a dark stain spreading across his leg.

Her father had shot his own security man.

Within moments, the police and FBI had arrested everyone in the house, including her father and George McCormick, Vanessa's father. Christy had only ever seen the man twice. He hadn't inspired warm fuzzy feelings. As he was loaded into a police cruiser, he glared at her, his gaze sending ice down her spine.

That stare was filled with hate and loathing.

"*Cumme*, Christy. Let's go home."

Home. It meant something different to the two of them. She wished it weren't so, but didn't think it would change.

"I want to see Ellie." She ached to hug her little girl, to tell her everything was fine.

"*Jah*, I know you do." Sam hadn't removed his coat, or his arm, from around her. They moved toward Sergeant Dawson's vehicle. "She's with Abram and Katie. When I saw her, she was fine." He hesitated. "I didn't tell her you'd been taken. I couldn't. I was holding on to hope so hard. I hope I wasn't wrong."

She nodded. He was new to this parent stuff, but she couldn't argue with his decisions. "She's five. You didn't have enough information to give her. Why worry her?"

Relief crossed his face.

When they arrived at the cruiser, she chose the back seat. "I'm going to close my eyes. If I snore, I don't care."

He grinned then kissed her cheek before she ducked

into the car. He was being mighty affectionate this morning, she thought and then scolded herself to not get used to it. She was going back to Columbus when this was through.

Christy refused to refer to it as home. It hadn't been home for years, and that wasn't going to change.

She had been joking about snoring, but once the car started moving, she couldn't stay awake. She didn't awaken until they pulled into the police station lot. Yawning, she exited the police car and handed Sam back his coat. "Thanks."

He looked like he wanted to protest. Instead, he swung it around and put his arms into the sleeves. "Glad I could help."

Sergeant Dawson led them inside the station and into the conference room. "You'll need to write out a statement," she informed Christy. "Every detail—no matter how small—regarding what happened, will help us."

Christy sat at the table. The sergeant provided her with paper, a couple of pens and a fresh cup of coffee. Christy reached for the coffee first. She drank her first sip and sighed. "I needed this. Thanks."

"You're welcome. I sent Hendricks to grab you a bagel or something to eat."

When the officer set a breakfast sandwich in front of her, Christy inhaled it. It had been over twelve hours since she'd last eaten. Although there'd been canned goods and water in the shelter, she had been unable to eat or drink. Her stomach had been tied up in knots the entire time.

Sam settled into the chair next to her. She smiled at him and picked up the pen to begin writing. The door opened. Glancing up, her jaw dropped. Her father, together with an FBI agent, entered, both carrying coffee cups.

"May we?" The agent pulled out a chair. She watched, stunned as the two joined her at the table.

"Hey, what's this, Jack?" Sergeant Dawson demanded. Interesting. She knew the FBI man.

"Nicole. Good to see you again." The Fed flashed a smile at her. "I'm glad it's you working the case. Anyway, there are some things I think you all should know… Patrick?"

Her father nodded his agreement.

Christy caught Sam's raised eyebrow and shook her head. She had no idea what was going on.

"So…" her father began, his face drawn and tired. "Christy, let me apologize for the past seventeen years. I've been a jerk—and it was deliberate."

He rubbed his chin. "When your mother disappeared, I knew something was wrong. She and I were in love. Why would she leave?"

Christy avoided looking at Sam as a pit opened up in her stomach. The breakfast sandwich she'd eaten turned leaden in her gut as her father continued.

"After a while, I had to admit it looked like she'd left me. I was in a bad way. My business was struggling. I had two small daughters at home. On the advice of my attorney, I divorced her, citing abandonment. Later, I met Vanessa. I thought by accident, but I was wrong."

He took a sip of coffee. His hand was shaking. "I don't know how it happened. Maybe it was my grief. But before I knew it, I was married to her. She convinced me to take out a loan from her father to keep my business afloat. It wasn't until it was too late that I realized her father was a mobster, in the very real sense of the word. Along with money, I also ended up with a crew of security people—" he made air quotes "—including Bryce and the man you identified as Dr. Simms."

The FBI agent set a group of pictures on the table.

Christy gasped and pointed at one. "That's the guy who chased me when I left. And him." She pointed out another picture. "He was following us."

"The ATVs," Sam murmured.

Her father set his coffee down and pushed it away. "They took over my business, used it to front their criminal activities. It wasn't long before I realized I'd been set up. I have no doubt George McCormick killed your mother, although I have no proof. You and your sister were threatened. I had to distance myself from you to keep you unaware, so you wouldn't stumble into anything. I had a tracker put in both your and Jo Anne's phones so I knew where you were. That's how I found you when you left."

"That's why you had Jo Anne brought home," Christy realized. "So you could watch her."

He nodded. "I knew that you were an undercover cop, Sergeant. I had been informed that someone was being sent in to investigate after I contacted the authorities."

"You called the cops?" she blurted.

"I did," her father confirmed. "I knew Jo Anne didn't overdose. It was clear how bitterly I'd failed to protect you both and needed help."

"We had to keep Patrick out of it as much as possible. If they knew he'd gone to the cops, he'd have been dead within hours, and so would his children."

It had all been to protect them. Christy couldn't take it all in.

"Jo Anne."

"I think she must have confronted someone, or said something. I'm not sure what put her on their radar."

For the first time, tears filled her father's glance. "To listen to people insisting that she'd been secretly on drugs, it was all I could do to hold it together. Jo Anne had never taken drugs. I knew it. My father-in-law and his minions also knew it. They destroyed a beautiful life so they could keep their operation going. It was the last straw."

She could barely take it all in. Sam reached over and took her hand. She needed his strength right now. She squeezed to let him know she appreciated it.

"Why did you kidnap me?" If what he was saying was true, it made no sense. "You locked me in a cellar, and it was cold there. I want to know why."

He met her gaze. "I knew they were closing in on you. I had been tracking you until your phone disappeared. But I knew something they didn't. I knew about Sam."

She paled.

"I knew who Ellie's father was. I found you the first time, remember? I made sure I knew all the details. So, I had an inkling where you'd go. I let you escape. George had put a hit on you the night Jo Anne was murdered. I would have let you be, but when Jack here—" he indicated the FBI agent "—told me about Sam being taken to the hospital and Simpson dying, I knew they'd found you. I brought you there hoping you'd be safe. I planned to tell you everything, but then Jack arrived. I knew he had information. He'd never have come to the farm if he hadn't. I had to hide you, just in case."

Just in case. Her whole world narrowed down to those words.

He'd emotionally abandoned them. Just in case.

She'd been trapped and controlled. Just in case.

She'd been kept in a bubble her whole life. Just in case.

She understood, but at the same time was having trouble processing everything. "So now what? Do we go home and pretend to have a normal life?"

She didn't even know what normal meant.

His face went a little grayer. "It's not that easy, my dear."

Jack leaned forward. "I'm sorry, Christy. Truly. But your dad, he's the only one with all the intimate details that can put George and his crew in prison for life. He has agreed to testify. But that means his life is in danger. We're putting him in protective custody. If you'd like to join him—"

She was already shaking her head. "No. I'm sorry, Dad. But I can't raise Ellie that way. She's lived in fear long enough. I want her to be a five-year-old. Not to be afraid to laugh or to talk too loud."

She bit her lip at the sadness on his face. She hadn't meant to hurt him, but her daughter was her priority.

"I understand. The house is actually yours."

"Mine!"

"Yes. It was your mother's, left to her by her grandfather. She left it to you and Jo Anne in her will. It became yours fully when you turned twenty-one. If you want to sell it, you can. Start somewhere new. Whatever you want."

She'd probably do exactly that.

Suddenly, she stood. "If you'll excuse me, I need some air to clear my head. I'll be back in a few."

Sam stood. "Should I—?"

She waved him back. "Stay here. I need a moment alone."

He didn't like it, she could see that. But he didn't protest. Now that the danger was done, Sam wouldn't hover. She had to appreciate a man who allowed her to do what she needed to do.

Leaving the room, she walked down the hall and stopped at the reception desk. "I'm leaving for a minute, just to walk around. I'll need to come back to finish my statement."

"Go ahead, honey." The woman smiled at her. "I'll buzz you through when you return."

She nearly ran to the door, desperate to be out of the building. She slowed her pace once she was outside. It was still brisk, but the sun was bright and inviting. She lifted her face and closed her eyes, enjoying the warmth on her skin.

It had been a long week. Losing her sister. Going on the run. Reuniting with her father. It was going to get harder before it got easier.

She remained for a few minutes before she straightened her shoulders and prepared to go back inside. She needed to face the rest of this conversation, then she could go and retrieve her daughter.

Thinking of Ellie brought a smile to her face. She turned. The smile fled.

"Hello, Christy." Vanessa casually held a gun close to her body. No one looking out would be able to see it. It was pointed directly at Christy's heart. "I think we need to have a chat."

SEVENTEEN

"Vanessa." Christy took a careful step toward her stepmother, stopping when the woman waved the gun at her. Vanessa stood tall and elegant, her makeup perfect and her blond hair smoothed into an intricate updo. She looked like she was ready for a fancy board meeting or a night at some upscale restaurant. Until you looked into her eyes. Pure malevolence gleamed from her blue orbs.

"Stay where you are, Christy." The sneer on Vanessa's face sent chills up her spine. "I'm not here for idle chit-chat. I have had all I can take from you. If it weren't for you, I'd be the richest woman in this town. As it stands, I've been mortified, and I have you to blame."

Ever since Vanessa had entered their lives, Christy had known the woman was cold and obsessed with her status and material wealth. She'd always had to have the best and newest of everything, from clothes to cars.

Never once, however, had Christy thought of her as a killer. Until now.

"You and your sister were so similar, weren't you? Neither of you could mind your own business. I had everything I wanted. Clothes, a beautiful home. My father was able to expand his business." She stepped closer to Christy. "And then you ran away, and life got even better. Jo Anne had inherited from her grandfather, so with you out of the way, I knew I would get the rest. I thought it would be so easy."

Her face skewed into an angry scowl. "But your father wouldn't challenge your mother's will. He said that it was her wish that you would have the house. Imagine that. You had run, and your father was telling me that the house I lived in would go to you when he was gone. The insult! I had planned on killing you then, I'd even sent out some men to bring you back. Your father got to you first."

Suddenly Christy understood. She remembered his threats, the way he never let her or Ellie out of his sight. Even the fact that he'd tapped her cell phone made sense in a morbid way.

"My dad found me and dragged me back. He kept me a virtual prisoner, to protect me from you, didn't he?"

Vanessa smiled at her like she was a child who'd done something clever for the first time. It made her sick to her stomach. The woman was pure evil.

"That's right. He even had a tracker placed in your phone. Can you imagine? He thought I didn't know. It didn't take much to trace it. It led me right to you."

It was Vanessa who had sent Simms and Bryce after her when she'd run. Her dad had come after her, too, but he'd only been trying to rescue her from Vanessa.

This was unreal. It was hard to believe anyone was this cold and calculated. She'd lived with the woman for seventeen years and hadn't understood how desperate she was.

She thought back to Jo Anne. She'd always known her sister hadn't overdosed. Not without help.

"Why Jo Anne?" Christy demanded. "She'd been so weak from cancer, what could she do to you?"

Vanessa barked out an angry laugh. "Why Jo Anne?" she mimicked. "Who do you think put her in the coma? I had been ready for her to die naturally so I could claim her inheritance, but then she got better. And when she got better, she started snooping. I saw her do it. I knew it was only a matter of time before she went to the police. Or her father. I couldn't have that, so I took care of it."

"You messed up, didn't you?"

Oh, Vanessa didn't like that at all. Fury sparked from her eyes. "I didn't mess up. Those idiots I hired did. Your father got suspicious, though, and hired round-the-clock help. It took me too long to find a way through his protections."

"She woke up," Christy remembered.

"She left me no choice at that point." Vanessa tilted her head. "You know, if you'd left well enough alone, I might have spared you. But because of you, I've lost everything. My father's on his way to jail. I can't go home. My bank accounts have been frozen. It's such a shame. After all I went through to get your father, and now it's come to this."

Something about the way she phrased it made Christy's blood run cold. "What do you mean what you went through? You met my dad at a business function."

Her light, tinkling laugh churned Christy's stomach. "Dear stepdaughter. Do you still believe your mother happened to disappear? I saw your dad before he married her and knew he was the one for me. She stole him. I just stole him back."

Christy swayed on her feet. It was suddenly very clear to her exactly what had happened. "You killed her. You killed my mother."

She didn't know the results of the DNA tests yet, but when they came back, she knew they'd prove the Jane Doe was her mother, and she was staring at her murderer.

"You know what? I'm done talking. We're wasting time here." Vanessa moved until the gun was inches from Christy's temple.

Christy swallowed. After all she'd gone through, she was going to die in a parking lot. After she'd finally found her father again and learned the truth about why he'd rejected any closeness to his children in all those years.

She hadn't even had a chance to tell him that she forgave him.

She wasn't about to die this way. She ducked her head and charged at Vanessa, hitting her in the chest. The taller woman teetered on her ridiculous heels. Christy used the time to make her getaway, spinning and running between the cars. She kept low, trying to make herself a smaller target.

The first shot went wide, smashing into a car window one vehicle over. The alarm rent the air. At least she wasn't a skilled shooter.

The second shot went wide.

The third shot… The third shot came from in front of her. Skidding to a stop, Christie saw Officer Hendricks standing there, his gaze locked behind her. Spinning on her heel, she froze.

Vanessa was lying on the pavement. Officer Hendricks stepped up to the prone woman and checked for a pulse.

"She's alive." He glanced up at Christy. "She'll probably spend the rest of her life behind bars."

Christy wouldn't be in danger any longer.

"Christy!" Sam ran over to where she was standing, her face white with shock. She let him tuck her under his arm and gently guide her toward his buggy.

She was shivering. "It's okay, Christy. You're safe now. She can't ever harm you or your family again."

She nodded. "Sam, I need to see Ellie."

"Of course you do. We'll go and get her right now."

He helped her up into the buggy. She sat beside him, staring straight ahead, her gaze pensive. The deep sadness in her demeanor gave him a hollow feeling in his chest. Some experiences took their toll on a person. Some people never healed from them. Look at Levi. Sam knew he'd had flashbacks when he'd come home from the military. It had taken him years to really get back to being himself.

In some ways, he never would be the same.

How would Christy ever recover from what she had been through? And not just the personal attacks. Those were traumatic enough. He'd heard what her father had said. He'd come around the corner right before the shots were fired, in time to hear the tail end of Vanessa's vile rant.

"She's taken my family from me. Jo Anne. Both my parents. She's taken them all from me."

He glanced at her, concerned. "You've still got your *daed.*"

She shook her head, the muscles in her throat and jaw working. "I don't. Not really. Because of her and her awful father, my father made himself into a monster so we'd not get close to him. I have no happy memories of my dad from the time I was six until today. And now, I finally understand, and he's going into witness protection so he can testify against George McCormick. I won't be able to see him, talk to him. Nothing."

Sam was sorry that she was losing the chance to reconnect with her father. At the same time, he was glad he wouldn't completely lose his daughter and Christy.

But what happened now?

He wanted so badly to ask her to stay. He wouldn't, though. If she stayed, she'd have to change and become Amish. She'd already dealt with too much change today.

They stopped by Abram's and picked up Ellie. She ran to her mother and kissed her. Only then did Christy seem to thaw a bit. Her shoulders sagged and she pressed her forehead against her daughter's.

Ellie said goodbye to her *aenti* Katie and *onkel* Abram and let Sam lift her up into the buggy.

He caught Abram's glance. When he saw the concern, he lifted his hands. He didn't know what to say or what would happen. He was just going to be happy that his family was safe.

He knew he should take them back to Abram's *haus*. He couldn't do it, though. Christy had nearly died.

Ellie chattered the entire drive to his *haus*. He wasn't sure how much Christy was listening, so it was a *gut* thing only noncommittal sounds were required.

He'd never seen a person as exhausted as she was.

Every now and then, her face scrunched up. He kept feeling like she was getting ready to cry. But she never did. Somehow, the way that she was holding all of her emotions in scared him more than if she would've screamed and hollered.

It wasn't healthy. It reminded him of how Levi had held himself back when he'd first returned.

It made sense. In a way, both of them had seen a sort of war.

When they approached his parents' home, he maneuvered the mare and buggy into the driveway and out beyond the *haus*. He needed to unhitch the horse and put her away, but he also needed to take care of Christy and Ellie. He slowed the speed of the buggy because Christy was so shell-shocked he wanted to disturb her as little as possible.

David came out of the house as they were pulling in. He met them by the barn.

"Sam, you get the girls into the house. Fannie has some food prepared. Take care of them. I'll take care of the horse and buggy."

Sam nodded, too grateful for words. He hopped down then turned to escort Christy off the buggy.

"Daddy! Help me, Daddy." Ellie waited, fidgeting inside the buggy. She'd found Stella and was clutching the doll in her arms. Tenderness welled up inside him for the child. Opening the buggy door, he lifted her down.

"Why don't we go inside and see what *grossmammi* has ready to eat?" he said, gently chucking her under the chin. She giggled. Sam slid his arm around Christy. Ellie ran ahead, calling for her grandmother and announcing that she was home with her mommy and daddy.

Fannie came to the back door. Her smile was quizzical as she took in Christy's pale, frozen expression. Her kind face softened in sympathy. She didn't press for details. Both of his parents were discreet and capable of reading others. They knew that Christy had had about all she could take.

Ushering Christy and Ellie into the *haus*, she set about getting them something to eat. Sam joined them, his stomach letting out a low rumble as he sat across from Christy. Ellie wasn't hungry, having been with Katie all day. She was happy to stay at the table with her parents, though.

Christy didn't eat much, although he was glad to see her drink a glass and a half of water. He hadn't said anything, but he'd seen how white her tongue had looked. Knowing that to be a sign of dehydration, he refilled her glass when he saw it was getting low.

When she put the glass down, she looked up at him.

She shuddered, her whole body shaking.

He looked at his *daed*. The older man stood. "*Cumme*, Ellie. Let's go into the other room."

Ellie stood, eager to be done with her meal.

His parents both left the room, taking Ellie with them. They went slowly, as Fannie's arthritis made it hard for her to walk. Ellie raced ahead of them.

By the time they had gone, the tears had started to spill over Christy's lashes and onto her cheeks. Christy didn't move to stop them. Her body was shuddering so hard, she looked like she was going to shatter. Sam scooted his chair back and rounded the table. Getting on his knees beside her chair, he gently took her in his arms.

She didn't resist. Laying her head on his shoulder, she wept. He ran his hand up and down her back in wide circles, trying to calm her. He didn't say anything; he just let her work her sorrow out of her system.

Had she really grieved for her sister yet?

He knew this was more than grief for Jo Anne. She was mourning her mother all over again, as well as her father. He couldn't imagine how hard it was, dealing with the losses she'd faced today.

Sam had no idea how long they stayed in that position. His knees began to protest. He ignored them. Giving her what she needed was more important than a little physical discomfort.

When she stirred, indicating she wanted to move, he released her and sat back on his heels.

She straightened and scrubbed her wet cheeks with her palms.

"Thanks." She smiled at him, a soft, sad kind of smile. "I'm tired."

Standing, he nodded.

"We won't make you leave tonight," Fannie said in her gentle voice. "It will be enough for you to sleep in the spare bedroom upstairs."

"I'll show you to the room," David offered. Christy stepped close to Sam and kissed him whisper-soft on his cheek. It wasn't a romantic gesture. It was a silent token of her appreciation for his care.

He couldn't do less for her. She held his heart in her hands.

And he knew, without her saying anything, that she was going to break it.

* * *

Sam didn't see Christy again until the next morning. He'd stayed back from work, knowing he couldn't face the day until he'd seen her.

Would she leave?

Why would she stay? He had wrestled with his decision not to ask her to stay all night. He knew she loved him. He might have been able to convince her to remain, to try to see if the Amish life was one she could do for a lifetime, rather than a handful of days.

In the end, he acknowledged that now was not the time to present such a question.

"Sam." His *daed* asked the question. "What are your intentions?"

Sam reverted to Pennsylvania Dutch, keeping the conversation private in case she came near enough to hear. "I have none. I love her. I said as much to Abram. But I can't pressure her. I can only trust, like you said, that all will be well, and *Gott*'s plan will win."

His *daed* took a careful sip of his *koffee*. It was still piping hot. "I'm proud of you, *sohn*. You've done what was right, even though it might cause you pain. You've handled yourself well."

He sipped his own beverage. *"Danke."*

He watched as his father put his hat on his head and slipped on his coat. The older man patted him on the shoulder before leaving the *haus*.

It was eight thirty when Ellie and Christy entered the room. Christy's eyes zeroed in on him. He didn't like the resolve he saw there. She was wearing the clothes she'd arrived in. His heart sank. While she was dressed Amish, part of him could pretend. There was no fooling himself when faced with his very *Englisch* wife.

"We need to talk, Sam."

He nodded, dread curling in the pit of his stomach.

Fannie gave him a look. He gestured toward the living room. Christy led the way. Behind them, Fannie was making Ellie giggle as she sat at the table to eat.

Arriving in the living room, Christy moved to the large picture window. She stood in front of it for a moment, her arms crossed over her stomach. He waited. Finally, she sighed and pivoted to face him.

"You already know what I'm going to tell you."

He grimaced. "You're leaving. Going back to Columbus."

He could practically feel his heart ripping in his chest. "I love you."

He hadn't planned to say it. It just slipped out.

"I know." She stepped closer. "I love you, too. But I'm really confused right now. I can't deal with this thing between us. Not yet. I know when the DNA results come in... I know they'll say that body is my mother's. But until I get them back..."

She looked at the floor. Her dark hair fell forward, making a curtain.

He reached up and tucked her hair behind one ear so he could see her face. "Do you want me to come with you?" And what? He wouldn't fit in her world. He just hated thinking of her alone in that *haus* where so much pain had occurred.

"No. But I appreciate it."

"How will you live in that *haus*?"

"I hate the idea. But I will go back and get it ready

to sell. I won't live there forever. As soon as I can, Ellie and I will move out."

There was nothing more he could say to her.

"Will I ever see you again?"

She hesitated. "Yeah. You have a daughter, right? We'll visit. I'm not going to keep her from you. A girl needs her father in her life."

He heard what she didn't say. A father that would love her and cherish her. Not like hers had done, even if it had been for her own protection.

"I'll miss you, Sam. Every hour of every day. But you know we don't have a future."

He nodded.

Two hours later, her ride showed up. He hugged Ellie. She cried, but he promised he'd see her soon. He settled her into the safety seat and stepped back from the car. She tucked Stella under her arm and waved at him through the car window. He didn't touch Christy. Neither did she move to touch him. He wondered if she was thinking the same thing. One touch, and he'd be begging her to stay.

In the end, he stood in the driveway, alone, as his child and the only woman he'd ever love departed.

EIGHTEEN

"Christy, this is Sergeant Dawson from the Sutter Springs Police Department."

Christy held her breath at the familiar voice. It had been three weeks since she'd left Sutter Springs. She'd returned to an empty home. Her father was in witness protection and her stepmother was in jail, as was Vanessa's father. It was just her and Ellie.

Each day had dragged by, consumed as she was with thoughts of Sam and his family—and what their life might have been. Her daughter missed Sam, too. Although, he had sent her letters. She'd promised him she'd bring Ellie to visit after everything was worked out.

Her heart ached to see him. She remembered his kiss. If she concentrated, she could feel the touch of his lips on hers. It wasn't enough, but it had to be.

She knew what the officer was calling about. Dread and hope warred inside her breast. She wanted to know. And at the same time, she was desperate to stall.

Enough. She needed to know, to carry on.

"Is it her? Is the body my mom's?" She bit her lip and waited.

Sergeant Dawson didn't drag out the suspense. "I'm sorry, Christy, but it is."

Tears filled her eyes and wet her cheeks. How she wished Sam were here!

"What do I need to do?"

For the next hour, she made phone calls and plans. The body would need to be transferred. The plot next to Jo Anne's grave had also been purchased by her father. She didn't know who he'd expected to be buried there, but it didn't matter. He was in witness protection and wouldn't be needing it.

In the end, it was a cold January day when Margaret O'Malley was laid to rest beside her oldest daughter. There were no other mourners besides Christy and Ellie. No one to commiserate and share memories with.

Ellie leaned against Christy. She played with her daughter's long curls as the minister finished the prayers over her mother's casket.

Within a few days, the headstone was in place. On a cold Thursday morning, Christy brought flowers to place on the grave. She'd expected to feel some sense of closure or finality once her mother was buried. Instead, she was empty inside. She stood looking at the tombstone as the snow fell around her, mingling in her unbound hair. She couldn't even cry anymore. She'd mourned her mom since she was six.

Her mother wasn't there. She would never see her again. At least not on this earth. Jo Anne was gone, too. And the father who had finally come back to her at the very end, the man who'd made his family fear him to protect them, was unreachable.

They were alone.

She'd lost everyone from her family.

Sam's face appeared before her. The overwhelming love that she'd tried to deny welled up in her heart. It overpowered her so that she couldn't breathe. The ache in her chest bent her over at the waist.

"Sam. Sam." She gasped out his name. Why had she given up on them so soon? He loved her. He loved Ellie.

She wasn't Amish. That was why.

But she could be.

Her house was on the market. There was already a prospective buyer. She had nothing she needed to remain here in Columbus for.

For the first time, she allowed herself to consider such a drastic step. She had spent several days with his family. She'd learned to believe again. After her father had rescued her and the danger had passed, she'd thought there was no reason to stay. It had just about destroyed her, but she'd returned to her father's house, even though he wasn't there anymore, and immediately had missed the simplicity of their life.

Yes, it would be a hard life. She'd seen the long days that Katie and Lilah put in. That being said, she'd have everything she needed. She would have her husband, her daughter and a family she knew she could grow to love as much as if they'd always been hers. Plus, she would belong to a community that helped each other in times of need. Whereas, when she'd needed help before, there'd been no one in her life to turn to.

And, probably most important, she'd belong to a church that tried to follow God in everything. That alone would give her life purpose.

The rightness of it struck her.

Running back to the house, she began to pack things for a few days for her and Ellie. Most of her belongings she'd have no use for. If she could convince Sam that she was serious, she'd have little need for the majority of her possessions. But first she'd have to persuade him.

That was the one sticking point. Would Sam want her? She knew he loved her, but she'd left him once. He might be reluctant to trust her again.

She paused in her packing. Was she setting herself up for heartache? Maybe. But she knew her current life wouldn't bring her happiness. She would miss Sam for the rest of her life. They'd been apart for six years, and no one had ever filled the hole in her heart caused by their separation. He was worth fighting for. She'd never know if she didn't try.

She finished packing and went next door to pick up Ellie. Her neighbor had agreed to watch her while Christy was out. She could hardly wait to get started on the new adventure spinning in her mind.

How much should she say?

She didn't want to disappoint her little girl. If Sam didn't want to give them a second chance, she'd be devastated, of course. But Ellie didn't need to know why they were going. At least, not the whole reason.

Ellie chattered the entire walk from the neighbor's house to theirs. When she saw the suitcases in the hall, she stopped. Christy had placed Ellie's doll on top.

"Mommy, why is Stella down here?"

Christy crouched in front of her daughter. "I thought we'd go on a little trip, honey. How do you feel about going to visit Daddy for a day or two?"

As soon as the words were out of her mouth, Ellie

squealed and threw her arms around Christy's neck. "Yay! We're going to see Daddy! Will we see *Grossmammi* and *Grossdawdi*? And *Onkel* Abram and *Onkel* Levi?"

She grinned at Ellie. "I'm surprised you didn't ask about Harrison and Barbara."

"Them, too, Mommy!" Ellie was bouncing with excitement. "And *Aenti* Lilah and *Aenti* Katie. When can we go, Mommy? Can we go now? Please, can we?"

Christy laughed. "Yes, we'll go now. We can be there in a few hours."

Carrying the bags to the car, Christy opened the door so Ellie could climb up in her booster seat. Christy stored the bags in the trunk and then got behind the wheel. It was a struggle not to push her foot to the floor. If she had wings, she'd fly to Sam, so anxious was she to see him.

Soon, she told herself. She'd be with her beloved soon. And then she'd know if he was ready to take a leap of faith with her.

She frowned. It might behoove her to see the bishop first. If she went to Sam and then the bishop said it wasn't possible, she'd break both their hearts. Her heart pounded inside her chest. The blood pumping in her ears nearly drowned out Ellie's constant questions.

She answered as best she could.

"Hey, Ellie-lu. We're going to stop to see Bishop Hershberger first, okay, honey?"

Her daughter wasn't impressed, but she must have seen something in her mother's face that made her hold back her complaint. Christy was determined to do this right. It was the most important decision she'd made, and it would affect the futures of her, Sam and Ellie, so she needed to do it correctly.

Needing strength, she spent the next few miles deep in prayer, asking for guidance and perseverance.

Suddenly, she was flooded with a sense of peace and purpose. She smiled and nudged the gas pedal with her toes.

She could hardly wait to see what this day brought. Her fear was gone. No matter what happened, she knew God was on her side.

Sam climbed up the ladder and dipped his brush into the burnt-orange paint. It was a hideous color in his opinion, but it was what the client wanted. His *daed* and Abram were working on a job at another site. He'd volunteered to take this one.

Neither of them had said anything, but he'd seen their concern.

He'd started asking for the jobs that could be done by one man. Because he didn't want to have to work with the others. He wasn't angry with anyone. Far from it. He needed solitude, though. Whenever he was with others, he felt caged in.

It was especially bad if he were with his brothers and their wives. While he liked both of his sisters-in-law, seeing the bonds of love and affection they shared with Abram and Levi was akin to holding his hands over an open flame to see how much pain he could handle. And watching his brothers with their *kinder*... Ack.

It had been four long weeks since he'd seen his Christy and Ellie. Four long weeks of working at a frenzied pace each day just so he could sleep at night.

Then dreaming of Christy every night and waking to the knowledge that she was gone and he hadn't fought for her.

He'd wanted to, but what would have been the use? He couldn't leave the church. Amish was who he was. Nor could he ask her to give up the *Englisch* world for him. His life was not one many born outside an Amish community could successfully take on.

Nee. He couldn't ask that of his feisty Christy. As much as he loved her, he couldn't ask her to change for him. It wouldn't be fair. He didn't know how he'd get through, though. He held tight to his faith. Not every story could have a happy ending.

He finished the first coat and backed down the ladder, then stepped into the center of the room to inspect his work. It looked decent. Well, as decent as burnt-orange walls could look. He grimaced.

Outside, the clop of hooves and the sound of buggy wheels pulling into the driveway caught his attention. He frowned. He wasn't expecting anyone. He glanced out the window and saw Levi's mare. Huh. Why was Levi here? His brother wasn't in the painting business.

Sam shrugged. Whatever. His brother had *gut* timing. He needed to let the paint dry before starting the second coat. The owners wanted the rooms all painted by the end of the month so they could move in. He'd been so driven these past few weeks that he was ahead of schedule.

That meant he'd soon have to find another project to occupy his mind. He sighed, letting his shoulders droop under the weight of his sorrow for a second before he forced himself to stand upright. He would bear whatever burden *Gott* handed him.

"I'm upstairs, Levi!" he called out. Might as well get this over with.

He heard running footsteps and frowned. Those weren't his brother's steps.

His breath caught as Christy burst into the room. He blinked. She couldn't be here. But she was.

In the space of two heartbeats, she was in his arms. He stopped thinking. He hugged her close, tears falling unheeded before he cupped her cheeks, wet with her tears, and brought his lips down on hers.

Any thought that he was dreaming disappeared at the taste of salt on her soft lips. The kiss deepened. He drew his head away for a moment, only to have her pull him back down.

Slowly, reason returned. He stepped back, though he couldn't find the strength to release her. Not yet. He couldn't bear the thought of letting her go.

"Christy, we can't… It's not right." His voice was harsh with longing.

"Dear Sam." Her voice was rich with emotion. "Darling, we need to talk."

The endearment was bittersweet to his ears. He longed to be her darling in fact, but couldn't see how it could ever be.

He brushed her tears away. "Christy, what are you doing here? Where's Ellie?"

She grinned up at him. "I left her with Lilah. Levi drove me here."

He heard the sound of a buggy leaving. His eyes widened. "Wait! Why's he leaving?"

She moved slightly to the side. He started to reach out to her again then stopped.

"He's leaving to give us time alone to talk."

"I'm working."

"I know. He says you're always working. And you are actually ahead of schedule, so I'm not to listen to your protests."

He laughed and scratched the back of his head. *Jah.* He could see Levi saying that. He gave in and stopped protesting. He stood there and looked at her, waiting for her to tell him why she had come, loving the way her brown eyes devoured his face.

"I don't know about you, but this past month has lasted for years."

He chuckled again. "*Jah*, it felt that way."

She nodded, satisfied. "Well, here's the thing. A few days ago, I learned that the body found was my mother."

He grimaced. "*Ack*, Christy. I'm sorry."

"Yeah. Me, too. I buried her on Saturday, next to Jo Anne. And with that, I put my past to rest."

What was she saying? She took one step nearer. He inhaled and the scent of her shampoo hit his senses like a balm.

"I've been praying a lot this month, Sam. I've found my faith. Actually, I let God catch me. I feel like He's been waiting for me to turn to Him. And when I did, I discovered something."

Another step.

"What was that?" His voice was little more than a whisper.

"I discovered that the world I lived in held no attraction for me. I don't care about fancy cars or houses, or nice dresses and fashion. I don't want to go to school and learn a new profession or to make a ton of money."

"What do you want, Christy?"

Now she was right in front of him.

"I want you, Sam. I want to raise our daughter together, and to one day add brothers and sisters."

"Christy, you know—"

"I do know. I also know that I've never been happier or more sure of myself than when I was here with you in your community."

He stopped breathing. "Christy, the Amish life is not easy."

She nodded. "I know it's not. But, Sam, the English world isn't easy, either. Especially when my heart is here with you. I love you, Sam. More than I ever did when we were seventeen."

He lifted a hand to her hair. "I love you, too, my Christy. But I'm not even sure if it's possible. Joining the Amish church isn't something you can do on a whim."

She snorted. "I know that. Which is why I visited Levi and your bishop before I came here."

This time, his laugh was a full belly laugh. She was one of a kind. When she decided to do something, she did it with gusto—that was for sure.

He smiled so wide, his cheeks hurt. "What did they say?"

She arched her eyebrow at him. "Your brother asked me what took me so long to come to my senses. The bishop was more serious. He quizzed me for a full hour and a half before he was convinced I knew what I was asking. He told me I'd need to take classes. We can't begin courting until I am officially part of the church. He repeated that several times, making sure I knew that even if I start learning about the Amish, I might change my mind."

"He's right."

She tilted her head back to look at him. "I know he is. But I also know that when I prayed about joining your church, I was completely at peace with the decision. This is where I am supposed to be."

He stepped back, putting several feet between them. The disappointment and hurt on her face made him hasten to explain. "If I stay close to you, I'll kiss you again. Since you're going to be Amish, you need to learn that when the bishop tells you something, you need to obey. If I stay close, I might forget."

Her smile returned. "That's going to be the hardest part. Knowing we can't kiss or hold hands or anything."

"*Jah.* But it will be worth it in the end."

"It will." She started. "Oh! Ellie is wild to see you again."

"I can't wait to see her, too. Let me take care of this painting, and we'll go to Levi's *haus* and collect our daughter."

She hugged herself, her brown eyes shining like stars. "Oh, Sam. I'm so happy! Happier than I can ever remember being."

As he finished up his painting, his heart was lighter than it had been since she'd left. They couldn't talk fast enough, trying to express everything that had passed since they'd been apart. It was as if they were trying to banish all the sad memories.

When he was done, she helped him clean up. This was how it would be, he thought. Working together, in tune with each other.

When they left, they drove to Levi's. Ellie ran out

to meet them. He swung her up in his arms, laughing as she shrieked with joy. His heart was full.

Lilah invited him to stay for dinner. He agreed with alacrity. Ellie ran ahead of them, eager to tell Harrison her daddy was back. He walked beside Christy, content. Her arm brushed his. He glanced down and met her eyes. It hadn't been accidental. He knew the joy on her face was a mirror of the happiness on his own.

He was more than happy. He was grateful that *Gott* had blessed them so much and answered their prayers.

They were going to get their happy ending, after all.

EPILOGUE

Nine months later

"**Y**ou're the prettiest Amish *maidel* I've ever seen."

Christy turned a smile at Sam, then held in a chuckle when she saw he was bowing to Ellie. Their daughter giggled into her hands and lifted her shoulders in pleasure.

"Daddy!" When she held up her arms, Sam swooped her up, grinning.

Christy blinked back a tear. She felt like she'd swallowed a sunbeam, the joy nearly overwhelmed her.

When he set Ellie back on her feet, she laughed and ran over to join the other children.

Sam turned his warm gaze on Christy. "And how are you? Any regrets?"

"Silly." She lightly batted his arm. "Of course not. I can't believe I'm finally a member of the Amish church. I'm so happy."

"Me, too."

They fell into step together as they walked around the field. The district had gathered together at Abram's house for church that morning. Christy breathed in deep, savoring the scents of delicious food, freshly mowed hay and the faint aroma of woodsmoke.

"I love fall." She deliberately allowed her arm to brush against his. She treasured these moments together. She'd been living with Abram and Katie for the past nine months. It wouldn't have been proper for her to stay in the same house with Sam. They were both determined to do everything the right way this time.

"Hmm. I can think of one major improvement, though."

She slanted a glance at him. A small smile played around his mouth. What was he thinking? "Oh? What improvement are you talking about?"

The smile grew to a grin. When he turned his full gaze on hers, she forgot to breathe as the wealth of love in his eyes warmed her. "If I could enjoy this season with my wife and my daughter in my *haus*."

Her heartbeat tripped. "We can't yet. Not until—"

"Not until we're married in the Amish church. What do you say, Christy? Should we make it official?"

"Can we? This quickly?"

"*Jah.* I talked with the bishop. We can be married in October, if you want."

"Oh." She clasped her hands and held them close to her chest as her dream loomed within her grasp. "We could celebrate Christmas as a family."

His eyes darkened. "*Jah.* I want that, Christy. I love you and Ellie so much. It's time to bring our family together."

"Sam, I love you, too. Yes, of course I'll marry you!"

He leaned forward and kissed her gently. It was more than a kiss. It was a promise.

* * *

"Mommy, is it time yet?"

Christy shoved the last pin in to hold her bun in place and turned to see Ellie silhouetted in the open door. Her daughter had sprouted so tall in the past year since they'd run from her father's house, she barely recognized her.

Standing, she walked over and folded the child into an embrace. Ellie snuggled close. Her hair was braided neatly, although it wasn't covered with her *kapp* yet. She treasured these private moments.

"Did Lilah do your hair for you this morning?" She squeezed her tight once before releasing her.

Ellie grinned up at her mother. "She did. It's fun having so many people in the house!" Ellie had been over the moon from the moment she'd learned getting married meant her daddy and mommy would live in the same house.

Chuckling, Christy kissed Ellie's cheek. Lilah and Katie were there, as was Sam's cousin Adele. The women had worked hard the past two days getting David and Fannie's house ready to host the wedding. Fannie was beyond thrilled that the ceremony and lunch would be happening there. She and David had moved into the *dawdi haus* the week before.

She heard feminine voices in the hall. Within seconds, both Katie and Lilah stood outside her door. They were to be her bridesmaids, or *newehockers*.

"Do you need any help, Christy?" Katie entered the room, Lilah right behind her.

Mentally running over the list of things she needed to do, Christy shook her head. "I think I'm good. Unless I've forgotten something, which is entirely possible. I seem to be having trouble focusing today."

Katie snickered. "I can't imagine why."

"If you did, Sam won't notice." Lilah motioned for Christy to slowly spin. She did so, feeling ridiculous. She wasn't wearing a fancy dress, although it was new. With the help of her soon-to-be sisters-in-law, mother-in-law and several cousins, she had managed to make her dress. It was deep blue, and she knew she'd be wearing it to church most church weeks. She'd never been so thankful that she'd learned to sew when she was younger! As the bride, she was supposed to sew the dresses of her attendants, too. However, Lilah, Katie and Adele had taken pity on her and sewn their own dresses.

"You're ready." Lilah nodded, satisfied.

"She is." Katie swooped in and gave her a gentle hug. "We're so glad you're joining the family. David and Fannie are happy to be in the *dawdi haus*. I think it was a relief, to Fannie especially, not to have the responsibility of the big house anymore."

"Yes," Christy said. "That's what she told me." Fannie had taken her under her wing as if she were her own daughter. She'd confided to Christy that her heart was overjoyed to see Sam getting married and taking over the family home. "She told me that David wasn't planning on retiring from the business yet, but he was pleased to know Sam and Abram would be running the place."

"*Jah*. It's a lot of work." Lilah nudged her toward the door. "Let's go get you married."

Butterflies zoomed in her stomach during the short trip to David and Fannie's house. She and Sam had been so young when they'd decided to get married over seven years ago. They'd been full of rebellion and unrealistic expectations. Neither had been ready for marriage.

She was ready now.

The ceremony itself was to be conducted in the larger barn where the family kept their business supplies. Sam and his brothers and father had cleared it out.

There was a small set of what looked like bleachers outside the barn. She paused. That hadn't been there yesterday. What was it for?

"Christy."

She gasped and swung around. "Dad?"

The other women melted into the background, giving them privacy. "Dad. What are you doing here?"

"I'm watching my daughter get married."

"But Vanessa's dad—"

He stepped closer. "I testified at George's trial last month. He's been sentenced. Both he and Vanessa will spend the rest of their lives in jail."

Her stomach clenched and her mouth went dry. How could he be so calm about this? Her entire life had been ruled by George's malice, regardless of whether she understood it or not, that man had been responsible for not only her mother's death, but also for the distance and coldness between her father and both of his children.

"Dad." Her throat closed. How could she even put this into words?

"Christy." Fresh tears welled up in her eyes at the tenderness in her father's voice. She couldn't remember his ever saying her name like that. "Everything will be well. George no longer has the power to hurt us. The police were also able to arrest some of his men. The cops now believe the danger to me and my family has been neutralized. I will regret for the rest of my life the way he and Vanessa damaged our relationship. I won't let them destroy the future. Today you're getting married to a fine man. You and he will raise my granddaughter, and any other children you have, and in a home filled with light, faith and love. If you let me, I would like to have a small part in your life."

Christy couldn't recall ever being the one to reach out to him. For as long as she could remember, such closeness had been discouraged. She did so now, stretching her arms out to embrace the father she had thought had been responsible for her sister's death. His arms closed around her, and a shudder ran through him.

God truly was amazing. She didn't know if she and her father would ever be truly close. But a new sense of peace settled in her heart as she finally got her father back.

Twenty minutes later, her heart was still singing as the ceremony that would permanently join her and her beloved Sam began. It was very similar to a regular church service. When it was over, however, she left as an Amish bride.

During the meal, she and Sam sat side by side at the table. Her bridesmaids sat beside her, while Sam's attendants filled the seats at his side.

"I hope no one asks me what I ate." She patted a cloth napkin to her lips. "I can't remember tasting anything, although I know I didn't eat much."

He laughed. "I'm sure they all understand. It was all delicious."

"You better say that." She gave a mock growl. "I helped cook it."

After they ate, they left the table so others could eat. That was one thing completely different from an *Englisch* wedding reception. The guests ate in waves. She'd also never expected to help cook the meal for her own wedding.

"I like the way you—I mean *we*—do this." She took the hand he reached out to her as they walked.

"What?"

"If we had a non-Amish wedding, I would have spent lots of money on a dress I'd never wear again. I would have had someone else cook the meal and bake the cake. I like that we were more than the guests of honor. We helped with every aspect."

He tightened his grip on her hand and she gave a gentle squeeze in response. "You haven't said anything about seeing your father here."

"I'm overwhelmed. I thought he'd have to go into witness protection for the rest of his life. I certainly never thought I'd see the day when I would have any sort of positive relationship with him."

"Our *kinder* will know both their *grossdawdis*."

She swallowed. "It will be some time before Ellie completely trusts him. She remembers how he was."

"*Jah.* It will take time. With *Gott*'s help, it will happen."

He turned to her, his gaze searching hers. His warm hands cupped her face. She shivered. "*Gott* has blessed us. I never thought I'd see you again. Nor could I move on."

Her hands crept up and curled around his wrists. "I will love you forever, Sam Burkholder. I hope we have many years together and are blessed with several sisters and brothers for Ellie."

"*Jah*, that would be *gut*. If it doesn't happen, though, I'll be content to have the woman I love and my sweet daughter back in my life."

As he lowered his head, she raised herself up on her toes to meet him halfway. When their lips met, she smiled against his mouth, eager to begin their journey together as the family God had meant them to be.

* * * * *

If you enjoyed this book, don't miss the other heart-stopping Amish adventures from Dana R. Lynn's Amish Country Justice series:

Plain Target
Plain Retribution
Amish Christmas Abduction
Amish Country Ambush
Amish Christmas Emergency
Guarding the Amish Midwife
Hidden in Amish Country
Plain Refuge
Deadly Amish Reunion
Amish Country Threats
Covert Amish Investigation

Available now from Love Inspired Suspense!
Find more great reads at www.LoveInspired.com.

Dear Reader,

Thank you for joining me for Sam's story, the last Burkholder brother. When I wrote Abram's story, *Covert Amish Investigation*, Sam and Abram had a conversation that sparked the question, what if Sam were already married? His wife would have to have had a strong reason for not joining him in Sutter Springs.

Then I wondered, what if his wife wasn't Amish?

That led me to Christy. She's strong and hasn't had an easy life. She needs to open her heart to let Sam in. Together, they face adversity, fall in love and learn to trust.

And then there's Ellie. I hope you loved that sweet and spunky little girl as much as I did!

I love connecting with readers! You can find me at www.danarlynn.com and sign up for my monthly newsletter to keep up with all my writing news.

Blessings,
Dana R. Lynn

WE HOPE YOU ENJOYED
THIS BOOK FROM

LOVE INSPIRED SUSPENSE
INSPIRATIONAL ROMANCE

Courage. Danger. Faith.

Find strength and determination in stories
of faith and love in the face of danger.

6 NEW BOOKS AVAILABLE EVERY MONTH!

SPECIAL EXCERPT FROM

♦

LOVE INSPIRED SUSPENSE

INSPIRATIONAL ROMANCE

*Someone will do anything to get federal judge
Sidney Logan to throw a trial—even target her
six-month-old foster daughter. And it's up to US deputy
marshal Tanner Wilcox to keep Sidney and little Lilly
safe. But with a possible mole in the courthouse,
trusting anyone could prove lethal…*

Read on for a sneak peek at
Rocky Mountain Standoff *by Laura Scott,
available January 2022 from Love Inspired Suspense.*

"Do you think I've been followed?"

Tanner hesitated, then decided he couldn't lie to Sidney. "Yes, I think so."

She shuddered. "I'm surprised Santiago's men didn't take a shot at me when I was standing outside Camella's doorway."

Yeah, that had been troubling him, too. Although it was clear that while Sidney was a target, the goal was to have her influence the outcome of the trial.

Something she couldn't do if she was dead.

Considering the amount of time it would take to bring another judge up to speed, he felt certain Santiago wouldn't want another postponement.

But then why kill Camella? Just to prove to Sidney how vulnerable she was?

Maybe, but in his mind, murdering the nanny didn't make any sense. Not if Santiago's men wanted to sway the outcome of the trial.

He shook his head and told himself that mystery wasn't his to solve. His sole responsibility was to keep Sidney and her daughter, Lilly, safe.

And he wouldn't mind some help. Using the hands-free functionality of his SUV, he called his boss, James Crane.

"Things are heating up in Cheyenne," Tanner informed him. "I could use some help."

"I can send Colt Nelson to assist," Crane offered. "Fill me in on what's going on."

Tanner quickly explained about the murder of Camella Monte and how he currently had Judge Logan and her young daughter with him. "We're heading to Fort Collins. Could you ask Colt to meet me there?"

"Yes. Keep me updated," Crane said.

Tanner disconnected the call when the crack of gunfire echoed around them.

"Get down!" he shouted at Sidney while he frantically searched for where the gunman was shooting from.

"Lilly!" she cried hoarsely.

"I know." Tanner was thankful the SUV hadn't been hit. At least, not yet. He wrenched the steering wheel and went cross-country, rocking and rolling over the rough terrain, toward the small town of Wellington, Colorado.

He was desperate to find a safe place.

Don't miss
Rocky Mountain Standoff *by Laura Scott,*
available January 2022 wherever
Love Inspired Suspense books and ebooks are sold.

LoveInspired.com